I0834690

SCRY OF LUST

Erotica by Members of the Kinky Writer's Munch
at Wicked Grounds in San Francisco

EDITOR

Sumiko Saulson

ICONOCLAST
PRODUCTIONS

EDITOR

Sumiko Saulson

ASSISTANT EDITOR

Mimi Heft

AUTHORS

Sumiko Saulson ◆ Lydia LaRue ◆ Serena Toxicat
Ouroboros Sings ◆ Charlee Verrette ◆ Lif ◆ Ev Joy Lokadottr
Francesca Gentille ◆ Merlin Monroe ◆ Kathleen Mahnke
Akasha Vampyrssa ◆ Sara the Black ◆ Max Silver

PROOFREADERS

Alexandria Vol ◆ Gorgon Zola ◆ Becka Robbins ◆ Rai Wells Jonathan Norton ◆ Chalice & Delight ◆Lydia LaRue
Tiffany Morris ◆ Bronica Blue

COVER ILLUSTRATION

Sumiko Saulson

COVER DESIGN

Mimi Heft

INTERIOR ILLUSTRATIONS

Leeloo Levay

ICONOCLAST PRODUCTIONS

ISBN: 9781094737478

ICONOCLAST
PRODUCTIONS

When Not To Try This at Home, Translucent Skin, Love, Spit And Pathos, My

ICONOCLAST PRODUCTIONS

DEDICATION

Profits from this collection are being donated to the San Francisco AIDS Walk, through SFGoth Team #5015, in memory of Gregory Matthew Hug.

ACKNOWLEDGMENTS

With thanks to *Wicked Grounds,* in San Francisco, for hosting the weekly Kinky Writer's Munch; *Octopus Literary Salon,* in Oakland, for hosting the book release party and AIDS Walk fundraiser; **SFGoth AIDS Walk Team #5105**; *SF Citadel,* where the writer's munch organizers Lydia and Sumiko met, *FetLife,* the forum for our online group, the members of the Bay Area kink community, who contributed to this effort with their writing, proofreading and moral support; and *Death Guild,* where we have our writer's after parties.

CONTENTS

DEDICATION....................4

ACKNOWLEDGMENTS....................5

CONTENTS....................6

CONTENT WARNING....................11

PREFACE: THE EMPOWERED USE OF FANTASY....................13

INTRO: WHEN NOT TO TRY THIS AT HOME....................15

THE PENETRATION OF ALBION....................19

VAMPETTE....................23

DOMINATION....................25

MY BELOVED GAVE ME A ROSE....................29

THE LEFTIST APPENDAGE....................30

PERSEPHONE'S PLEA....................34

ANDONA'S FEAST 36

REMOTE CONTROL 42

LETTER FOUND IN THE WRECK OF A PIRATE SHIP SUNK IN THE CARIBBEAN APRIL 10, 1947 48

CAN WE TAKE TURNS? SWITCH WITH ME? 50

A NEW SENSATION 52

THE PICNIC TABLE 55

TRANSLUCENT SKIN 57

ADUALITY {0≠2;1=108} 60

FOUR HAIKU 68

FIRESIDE LEGENDS 69

SPIT AND PATHOS 73

THE TRIP TO THE ABANDONED FACTORY 75

BETWEEN TWO ROOMS 84

*** * * 85**

*** * * 86**

TATAMI AND WOOD 89

BTLAZOLTEOTL IN THE LANGUAGE OF HINDUISM AND ASATRU 95

BEAU'S TURN 98

LOVE.......... 108

BIMBO SUTRA #2 115

OREOS.......... 118

THE CLEARING.......... 123

Part I 123

Part II 125

Part III 127

Part IV.......... 130

THE TURNING OF DESMOND.......... 133

THE CHASTENING OF JADE WOODS 135

GETTING HAMMERED 141

EGO: FREE ME 153

1 Pondering 153

2 Where Am I? 154

3 Who Am I? 154

4 Enlightened 155

5 Aftercare and Introspection 158

ABOUT THE AUTHORS...159

BOOK DESCRIPTION 162

Art by Leeloo Levay

CONTENT WARNING

AND A CONVERSATION WITH ANNE RICE

CONTENT WARNING: This book contains explicit sexual content, graphic language, and situations that some readers may find objectionable: queer sex, alien sex, elf sex, demon sex, Valkyrie sex, amphibiod sex, harpy sex, BDSM theme and elements, dubious consent, and fantasies of a kinky nature. Reader discretion is advised.

During the editor's process of determining whether or not the dubious consent (dubcon) label should be used to describe science-fiction and fantasy stories in the collection that involve mystical or magical coercion as a pretext to BDSM stories, she did a lot of research on the subject, and uncertain as to whether not the label applied here, the editor shot off an email to Anne Rice, author of the BDSM titles The Claiming of Sleeping Beauty, Beauty's Punishment, Beauty's Release, Beauty's Kingdom and Exit to Eden.

As the Sleeping Beauty Quartet use fantasy enslavement as a trope, she seemed to have some expertise on the matter.

So Sumiko Saulson sent off a message as follows;

"I know you are busy, but I have some stories in Scry of Lust - it is an anthology that I am putting together with a group of people I am more or less teaching how to write and publish BDSM erotica. We meet every Monday at Wicked Grounds Cafe in San Francisco, which is a kink themed coffee house that hosts a lot of munches or kinky meets, we are one of them.

Some of the stories have dubious consent situations and some, like Sleeping Beauty Series, have fantasy or sci-fi worlds where consent is mystically a non-issues but Smashwords also requires you to self-report involuntary sexual slavery. I don't think I will need to report mystical sexual slavery that is of dubious consent that way but I am listing it as dubious consent. Does that make sense?

I am very nervous about my anthology getting pulled over a demon forcing a girl to give him head."

Anne Rice, being a cool person as well as a talented crafter of kinky erotica, answered as follows:

"Hard for me to answer. Some people obviously enjoy the fantasy of being forced to submit to sexual attention, being captured & enslaved against their will. Both men and women enjoy this kind of fantasy. The captivity, the enslavement, the release from any responsibility in the fantasy for what they enjoy is key to them.

I celebrate the right of people to have that fantasy, and the freedom to write books for them, and their freedom, obviously, to write their own stories and books. I chose the fairytale matrix to escape the literal world of ugly headlines and criminal violence. I wrote the Beauty series, all four books for those who enjoy that kind of fantasy, voluptuous captivity in a lush environment where the slave is forced to enjoy ecstasy over and over again while others watch... The slave is often the center of attention, or certainly the magnet of the master or mistress's attention.

I sought to create a refuge in which the slave is safe, prized, gorgeous, seductive, "helpless" having climax after climax. Seems to me the books made it obvious that the "captives" loved it that the enslavement facilitated their surrender to the deep enjoyment of spanking, or being punished with paddles, belts, etc. and the thrill of being the center of attention as they experienced ecstasy over and over again. The limits are clear; the slaves are prized and valued. All slaves are consumed with sexual desire.

The fourth book in particular deals with the complexity of the fantasy, how it works, shifting into various points of view to examine the dynamic, and the dynamic of giving the slaves what they want.

I'm not sure dubious consent covers it.

What about "Fantasies of safe enslavement." What about a disclaimer before a story? "This is for those who demand a matrix of safe & delicious enslavement or voluptuous coercion." Could be abbreviated: "Safe Enslavement Matrix." "Captivity Matrix" "Enslavement Matrix" "Fantasy Enslavement Matrix."

Don't know what else to say."

PREFACE: THE EMPOWERED USE OF FANTASY

By Francesca Gentille
Clinical Sexologist & Director
The Somatic Integrative Healing Institute

Stir a shaman, a counselor, and a clinical sexologist together and you get a perspective on fantasy that may be a bit different. Back in the 1800s, Sigmund Freud viewed fantasy as a reflection of what might be unresolved in the psyche. For over 30,000 years, shamans have believed that there are multiple planes of reality that have equal value and merit. So dreamtime is equally important to daytime, messages from the ancestors equally valuable to messages on social media (if not more so), etcetera.

In over 30 years of being a Shaman, 20 years of being a clinician, and a decade of being a Priestess Domme and Tantric Submissive, I've come to view fantasy as a symbolic language of the soul. Fantasies, like dreams or daydreams, always arrive in service of our wholeness. However, the psyche speaks a pictorial language that is not one to one. What does that mean?

It means that if I fantasize about having sex on a chair, it might not mean I need to go out and get a chair and have sex on it. It could mean that it's time to reclaim my throne of power, or to rest, or to be supported or something else.

Even a nightmare comes in service of our wholeness. For example, I used to dream of vampires hunting or attacking me. By going back into the dream through Active Visualization I was able to meet the vampire and ask, "Who are you? What is your message for me?"

What I heard was "I am you. If you deny me, I will kill everything you love. But I am wise. I am charismatic. I can be a great ally. But you must acknowledge me, and you must feed me." That delving in rather than acting out, transformed the way I live my life.

Instead of pursuing the next new relationship high over and over, I was able to redesign my life to include sensual dance performance, to be able to receive the attention I craved and the seduction that I wanted to express in a manner that was safe for me and others.

Well, let's look more closely at fantasy. For instance, I'm a cuddle bunny who wishes I were reincarnated as someone's favorite pet. I love all the loving touch opportunities, and oodles of kissing as well. One day, I chose a partner who just wanted to fuck. No foreplay. No kissing. No caressing.

At first I was angry and resentful, but because I am Researcher of Life, I chose to partner with him to see if I could transform myself to receive what he was giving without making him wrong.

While we were making love I began to have a fantasy of being in a large Cathedral, on my knees, surrounded by a circle of Cardinals in red. In the vision, there is a lot of sucking and fucking going on.

This appeared each time we had sex. I began to wonder why. I asked myself "What do a Cathedral and Cardinals symbolize?" and "What is red to me?"

What I saw was these images represented the sacred Eros and vitality I was longing for. They represented a missing nutrient in my experience. As long as I chose to stay with B. I had this fantasy. Never before him. Never after.

There is an important distinction between Manifest Fantasy and Personal Fantasy. Manifest Fantasies are what we choose to bring into reality after analyzing the risk versus reward, the consent and collaboration potential, the intention and proposed outcome. Personal Fantasies are what we choose to focus upon while self pleasuring or engaging with another in pleasure.

The key is choice. If a fantasy or desire becomes overwhelming, overcoming, disconnective, or it takes us away from our lives, then perhaps we may wish to uncover the hidden message that the fantasy is trying to give us.

One way to work with fantasy is through the arts; to write about it, sing about it, dance about it, create a play or film about it, or something else. Channeling what is stirring within through creative expression can entertain, catalyze, and even ignite transformation. If we choose.

I honor each author in this anthology for their courage, passion, and vision. As you enter into the worlds of our psyches, I invite you to see what resonates with yours. May it soothe your soul, open your heart, inspire your mind, and nourish your Eros.

INTRO: WHEN NOT TO TRY THIS AT HOME

By Sumiko Saulson
Mauskaveli on FetLife
Author, Moderator of the Kinky Writer's Munch

When I first met my co-moderator Lydia LaRue, at the Citadel in San Francisco, we were in the middle of a kinky speed dating round at an event called – you guessed it! Kinky Speed Dating, hosted by PsychoKitty. We were instructed at the outset to be open to meeting cool new friends who weren't necessarily partners. In the next round I met someone named Merlin Monroe, who is now my submissive and also my polyamorous partner as we have been dating for three months, since that fateful day in January 2019.

Merlin is also Priestess' service submissive. Priestess wrote the preface in the book just before Introduction. So there was a certain synchronicity and fatefulness to that day that cause both the Kinky Writer's Group and this book to come into being. This demonstrates a key difference between real-life kinky people and much of kinky fantasy and erotica: community building.

Lifestyle kinky people exist in communities that are often absent from kink erotica. These communities provide safe spaces for kinky people. Dungeons like SF Citadel have dungeon masters and rules to make sure everyone stays safe. Organizations like Society of Janus help iron out disputes in the community.

Safe spaces like Wicked Grounds, where we hold the Kinky Writer's Munch meetings every Monday from 7pm to 8:30 pm, provide a place for people in the kink community to meet outside of play spaces like dungeons and build non-pickup centered relationships and deeper, lasting friendships, family and community.

My friend Rai Wells lives in a small college town and adds, "Outside of big cities like SF, LA, Detroit, NYC, etc, there may not be dungeons or munches, and even if the community is there it doesn't necessarily mean it's a safe community. If the community where you're at is nonexistent or not safe, finding like-minded kinksters online is also a valid form of community."

Forums like FetLife offer online community to Kinksters, and Rai has also found kinky community in social media groups on places like Facebook (where we met through Goth group friends) as well on vanilla dating sites.

In the world of fantasy, plot devices make it so that people can go straight to the romance-sex action, skipping past community. They involve characters who quickly jump into romances, BDSM scenes, and sexual intercourse, sometimes with minimal setup. Mystical or other forces intervene so the reader goes directly to pants-warming fantasy without pausing for any mood-breaking disclaimers about safety, sanity, and consensual behavior.

As a result, there has been a lot of talk around the kink community about how BDSM newbies are picking up copies of E.L. James' *50 Shades of Grey* and rushing into dodgy consent relationships ready-made for domestic violence and abusive behavior, because they think Christian Grey's micro-managing lifestyle contract and lack of safe words sound hot. E.L. James doesn't thoroughly address the power dynamics of age difference and domestic violence until a later book.

Authors aren't responsible for the actions of unethical dominants; however, domestic violence is a real problem both in and out of the kink community and warrants address. Those inexperienced with BDSM negotiation and relationships can get into hot water going from fantasy to reality without communities to keep them safe. It is extra important to use caution about consent when you are negotiating something like beating someone's ass with a wooden paddle until it bruises. The submissive has to be concerned about personal physical safety. The dominant has to be concerned about legal safety, as the law doesn't readily distinguish between consensual and non-consensual beatings. Both parties have to be concerned about things like aftercare and extended aftercare that relate to their emotional wellbeing.

Fantasy and erotica are not how-to-manuals for kinky sex. So where is the author's responsibility here? I would say, as the editor of this anthology, I encourage you to go to munches, get factual books that are instructional, and get involved with people who are knowledgeable and trustworthy before engaging in kinky encounters with people. Don't look at a fictional book as a how-to-manual.

If you are able to find a public space like a community center, cafe, or other safe public place in your community, meet prospective partners there, first — not at your home. If you aren't, make sure you have other safety measures in place, such as initial meetings in public vanilla (non-kinky) spaces and informing loved ones, just like with vanilla (non-kinky) dating.

And talk to some sensible people about what you plan to do.

This isn't meant to be a discouragement, but encouragement to play safe out there. By all means, whet your appetite with fantasies. Find out what you like, and explore. Don't be ashamed of them. But be safe in doing so.

There are kinky stories that are obviously fantasy – like Charlie Verrette's

The Penetration of Albion and Serena Toxicat's *The Leftist Appendage*. Then, there are stories like Lydia LaRue's *Domination* and Ouroboros Sings' *The Clearing* that don't involve any supernatural elements. It is important to remember that, just because there isn't any three-penii having sea amphibiods or demons who are thought to be gods, transgender Valkyries or bot alters in the story, that doesn't mean it isn't fantasy.

In a fantasy world like Anne Rice's *The Punishment of Sleeping Beauty* or John Norman's *Gor*, the reader is instantly clear on the fact that this isn't real life and is just spank bank material.

Stories that don't feature any elements of science-fiction or paranormal fantasy aren't necessarily autobiographical and shouldn't be presumed to be such. Pauline Réage's *The Story of O* is a fantasy even though all of the characters are human and it takes place on Earth. Some of these stories depict hardcore fantasies that lifestyle kinky folks do engage in, but most erotic fantasy short stories don't show the negotiation on screen. They either cut-screen and show the sub in shackles, or have a plot device that is quite often very dodgy in terms of consensuality, where the submissive naturally wants to submit because it is from a strange alien race of naturally submissive beings.

In real-life BDSM relationships, you can't just mind read like that.
You have to negotiate and come to agreements about consent in advance.

Now that we have that out of the way, please read and enjoy these very hot stories and have fun. But before you set out on this journey, be forewarned that there are graphic depictions of bondage, vanilla sex, kinky sex, dominance, submission, sadomasochism and sexualized violence in fantasy settings that are not intended to portray an idealized version of consensuality in BDSM.

Artwork by Leeloo Levay

THE PENETRATION OF ALBION

by Charlee Verrette

"Tally ho chaps!" I heard the familiar hunting call come through the radio speakers as I prepared to dive into the dark mass of Heinkle bombers beneath me. Bombers full of evil men who wanted to kill my family and girlfriend. My cannons were roaring and the sky was a place full of chaos, filled with exploding planes and men dangling from parachutes.

I had just scored a direct hit on a Heinkle, and was momentarily elated when I heard the words no pilot wants to hear.

"Albion, Bandit on your tail!"

The ME-109 was on me and closing in fast. Before I could even think I heard and felt the thud of cannon shells around me. I was hit and bleeding from several wounds in my leg, chest and head. My Hurricane fighter plane was on fire!

Immediately my thoughts went elsewhere, a sunny field with local farmers working, the smell of freshly baked bread, and the soft laughter of girls. But soon enough the reality of the moment set in. My Hurricane was on fire and headed nose down to England's fair pastures.

I was still alive when we hit the ground; the plucky war horse plane had not yet exploded. It was then, as we lay on the ground, shaking and burning, that I felt a most peculiar sensation. It was if all my senses were suddenly heightened, and a loud humming mixed in with the sounds of the flames devouring the Hurricane. There was something reassuring in the humming sound and I wanted to know what it was. It was then that I became aware of a looming figure by the plane. I assumed it was a Green Goddess rescue crew and felt a sense of relief.

I could barely see through the smoke and oil stained window canopy, but what I did see threatened to take away the remainder of my breath. It was a very tall and statuesque warrior dressed in the manner of a Viking's. I laughed, thinking surely I was hallucinating. Then a most unexpected thing happened. A hand covered in shimmering chainmail crashed through the canopy window and began clearing away the broken glass. My straps were cut away with a jewel encrusted ancient dagger. I was loose now, and wondering what was next.

The entire cockpit canopy housing was then ripped off of the plane and thrown to the ground by this powerful creature. The whole time this was happening the creature was on top of me, pressing down on my dying body. I felt both attracted and scared by this fantastic being that, to my utter amazement, sported a beautiful pair of wings. I was even more certain I was hallucinating!

I had been mortally wounded and bits of the fuselage were sharing space with bodily organs. I was losing blood fast, and soon would be dead. It was then I became less aware of my pain and more in sync with the intense hum which seemed to be filling me with curious sensations and new power. Next, I felt the hot, sweet breath of the winged creature next to my face and our eyes locked. My brain felt like it was being read like a book, I felt a buzzing behind my eyes. I then heard that great yet terrifying voice speak for the first time.

"I am Gollun and I am Valkyrie! The Aesir and Vanir bid you welcome in their halls!"

Valkyrie?! Yes I had indeed grown up seeing depictions of the flying warrior women, foot soldiers of Odin and Freya. Would I now be admitted to one of these mythical palaces? Well, I was a good Anglican and had no belief in old stories from ancient times. It was obvious I was expiring, and my sanity had been replaced by a dying man's madness.

Though I was rapidly feeling less pain I could still feel physical sensation and what happened next, though entirely fantastic, was straight out of the grandest myth. Great and powerful arms reached under my armpits and in one motion lifted me out of the soon to be exploding fighter plane. We shot upwards into the smoke and fire filled skies, past the tangle of engaged fighters and bombers.

I could see green fields and treetops. The flight was effortless to the Valkyrie, who held me tight in a bear hug. At a certain point we had reached a tremendous height and we were no longer flying, we were floating, intertwined in a ball of Valkyrie and fighter pilot. I felt nervous, scared and a little giddy. Gollun was running their hands over me, healing wounds and staunching blood flow. I held on tight to that firm and armored body, and was in awe of its power and beauty.

Then it happened... Gollun delicately kissed my lips and inserted a hot wet tongue into my mouth. I had very little experience with girls and like many of the lads was terrified to die a virgin. However, despite the pleasure and longing I felt I was sure I had gone completely insane as I was now experiencing being kissed and fondled by a magical being with wings. A magical being loaded to the hilt with advanced weaponry as well.

But who and/or what was this armored flying creature? A woman? Well, they did have beautiful long hair and huge breasts. But they also wore a codpiece! What was the codpiece for? And the voice was neither male nor female, just powerful and ancient. I was as confused as any nineteen year old chap would be. I felt sexually excited and while it was wonderful I felt conflicted and guilty. I just had held my dear Wendy, a Biggins Hill controller, in my arms the previous evening.

But all of that worry vanished as I became aware that the codpiece had vanished and a rather large and full penis was thrusting upwards from the groin of Gollun! I buried my face deep in Gollun's ample bosom and all the fear and pain melted. It felt like the first time I had heard 'Thus spake Zarathustra', a whole new world was opening up and I was dangling from its furthest ledge.

I was being probed, kneaded and caressed by powerful yet kind hands and I was doing the same in return. We were clutching each other madly and the humming sound seemed to be moving towards a crescendo. Gollun was focusing on my head and thrust two metal clad fingers into my mouth. I tasted blood and battle, this excited me greatly. I was ready to submit completely to Gollun. I was being probed, pulled, licked, consumed and I loved the aggressive attention.

The Valkyrie then forced my head down and soon I was eye to eye with a huge, throbbing cock that was literally moving on its own accord. It twitched with urgency and was both pretty and frightful. My tongue flew out of my mouth and soon was spreading sweetness over the Valkyrie cock. Jera Raidho Ansuz! Were ancient and powerful Gods directing this erotic ceremony unfolding over England's green pastures?

I was soon devouring the huge shaft, head bobbing up and down like a pump at a mill. Gollun groaned and clouds seemed to be moved by their heavy breaths. We certainly weren't floating anymore; we were flying at an incredible rate upwards. Gollun's cock seemed to press further and further into my throat and though I gagged it felt wonderful. My head had become one hot wet hole, happy to be occupied by the invading cock dragon.

I felt superb, conquered but content as the rooftops and manicured fields grew dimmer and farther away. Then Gollun withdrew and turned me around, pressing their cock against my ass. I felt neither shame nor fear, just a heavy desire to let this terrible but sweet creature turn me into a willing target for their pleasure. Next I felt Gollun's cockhead poking at my gate and I was elated.

I submitted and I was pierced and penetrated, gasping and breathless. I gave into the rhythm and began chanting runes which I really had not known till that moment. Raidho Jera Ansuz Sowilo Mannaz Ehwaz. I had become a happy go lucky flesh vessel for my Valkyrie lover and was ecstatic. The horror of the day's battle had come to an end and what a beautiful end it was.

Flesh, steel, oil and blood were exchanged freely and soon conclusions to the fiery lovemaking would be made. I felt extremely fast thrusts from Gollun and their loud groans drowned out the sounds of the passing bomber formations. Soon I felt a huge heat increase between Gollun and my skin, and then a felt a huge explosion shake my entire body until it became a fine dust mist.

I had been completely consumed and annihilated by the lust of the Valkyrie. We were no longer flying and for a bit I lost all sensation. I no longer felt the Valkyrie near me though I felt no discomfort or fear. I felt I had come home to the home of the Gods.

"Albion it's your move" said the old but virile one eyed man who hovered above the chessboard on an oak table in a huge library. Yes, this is how I spend my days now, playing chess with the Gods, drinking mead and continuing my new role as a wife to a Valkyrie lover!

VAMPETTE

By Francesca Gentille

My fingers drip
With life red blood

Your heart
Beats softly
In my palm

But still

I'm not yet
Satisfied

Though my lips
Have sucked
At love

More
I want MORE
Of IT

For a
TASTE
Of IT
I would sell
My soul

But

As one of the Forsaken
I lie

I WANT IT ALL!

DOMINATION

By Lydia LaRue

She lay on the floor, afraid to look at him as he loomed over her naked body.

He leered down at her, "You gonna be good for me, huh?"

She nodded, but he nudged her with his black boot.

"I can't hear you…" He prodded her thigh, digging the bottom of his boot into her flesh.

"Yes, sir." She raised herself up slightly, but only looked at his boot.

He kept his foot on her thigh, and then roughly slid it off. He went around her and prodded her ass, digging the toe into her.

"Come on, get up, and move." His tone was bored, as if he were chiding an old dog. Though he'd treat an old dog much better than he'd treat her.

She complied, and rose to her hands and knees, kneeling.

"Crawl", he drawled out lazily before he grabbed the riding crop. He whacked it against his leg a few times in warning. He looked down at her and shook his head. "You're not moving fast enough."

He moved to her before she could turn her head and shoved her ass with his boot again, enough to throw her off balance. "You're too slow."

He nudged her arm and pushed her, but as she tried to regain balance he brought his foot to her chest, boot toe touching below her collar bone as he moved to push her.

She grabbed his boot, but at the last second he pulled his foot from her and she fell forward.

She sighed in frustration but he threatened her.

"Uh uh! Not a peep from you." He brought the riding crop to her mouth, "Hold this, that'll keep your mouth still." He grabbed a handful of her hair as he bent down to her. He enjoyed the sight of her helpless and frustrated. He grinned at her.

She narrowed her eyes and a deep frown line appeared between her brows. Her lips wrapped awkwardly around the crop and her teeth bit down.

He could tell she was desperately trying not to drool. He let go of her hair and snapped his fingers as he turned. "Don't tell me you can't manage to crawl and hold the riding crop in your mouth at the same time." He mocked her.

She glared murderously at him. She hated his voice. Dripping like molasses and sharp humor on a stick. He was prodding her mercilessly. She crawled obediently to him and waited for his next command.

"Gimme that." He flashed his fingers, palm up and she spat the crop out.

"Eww! It's covered in drool, he complained, and wiped her saliva off it on her back. He raised the crop, "Ass in the air up high for me."

She raised her ass, kneeling while resting her head in her hands. Her cheeks were warm and most likely red with embarrassment.

He whipped the crop over her ass sharply. She winced and moaned.

"Oh I barely touched you." He scoffed, and then smacked her harder.

She winced again and moved slightly.

"Do not move while I whip you. Or I will whip you someplace, less pleasant." He almost sneered. He raised his hand and gave her ass a big smack.

She yelped but held still.

He smirked to himself. Oh joy! He began whipping her faster, on each ass cheek, on each side of her thigh and back to her ass again.

Then he ended with his two hands to her ass,

Smack!

She let out a terrible groan and sank down.

"What did I tell you?"

She moaned.

He bent down to her, lifting her up by her chin. "What did I say?"

"Don't move," she mumbled.

"But you did move, and now I'm going to have to punish you. You see how that works?" He raised the crop to her. "Lie down on your back, hands behind your head."

She slowly slumped into position. She looked up at him and felt his immense presence even more in this helpless position. With her arms behind her head, she waited with trepidation.

"Spread your legs." He ordered. His face was stern.

She spread them apart.

"That's not wide enough. Wider, still." He walked around and nudged her feet open with his boots. Now her legs were splayed in a rag-doll like position.

He stepped between her legs then reached for her pubis with the riding crop. He stroked down to tease her and he noted she was wet.

Good Girl...

He teased her a bit more, brushing the tip of the crop to her clit and circling it within the leather loop. He roughly scraped her clit with the loop then stepped back. "Bend your legs and bring your pelvis up to me. I want your cunt within easy reach." He raised the crop.

She hurriedly bent her legs, knees up and then lifted her hips up to meet him as he swung the crop and hit her right on her clit.

"Ahh, shit!" She swore and had to collapse down on the floor again, her hips hitting the floor with an ungraceful thud.

"Up!" He raised the crop. He licked his lower lip before biting it thoughtfully and her eyes watched his every move. He brought the crop down and hit her again on the front of her pubis.

She groaned but he continued. Her legs shook as he whipped her again and again.

With her pelvis still up and legs shaking he reached for her with his fingers. He brought his thumb over her clit as his middle finger entered her. His light ministrations brought her to the brink and her legs shook.

She pushed into his fingers again and again, finally whimpering as she came. She couldn't take anymore and she had brought her hands to his hand and held him. His other hand caressed her thigh--the crop now forgotten.

She squirted out her body fluids and it ran down her ass and dripped onto the floor in light viscous drops.

He released her and she collapsed down onto the floor. "Oh, I'm not done with you yet. Hold still…"

He undid his pants and with his hand still wet from her body fluids, stroked himself. He propped his boot on her thigh as she watched him through half-lidded eyes. His breath came out in fast pants as he worked himself into his fist, using his other hand to grasp his balls as he watched her splayed out on the floor.

He removed his boot and stepped over her body to crouch and bend down over her stomach. With one hand he stroked himself as his other hand slid down her chest and touched her breasts. He reached to her throat and held her in a possessive manner, feeling her swallow her saliva as she watched him.

He grinned and then chuckled out loud as he felt himself going to the edge of his climax. He closed his eyes and groaned, spilling out his cum onto her chest in white rivulets that covered her nipples and ran into the hollow of her throat.

"Ahh, that was so good." His spaced-out grin and soft laugh made her hot all over.

She moaned and brought her arms to him and he bent down to kiss her.

"Oh good girl." He purred to her, "You're all messy now."

"You gonna lick it up?" She challenged him.

He quirked a brow at her, then leaned over her and extended his tongue to her nipple. He licked then made a face at the taste.

"Payback, bitch." She snickered.

He swiped his own cum onto his fingers and smeared it over her mouth. "Who you callin' bitch? You cat. Catty-cat-cat!" He smeared more cum on her face and she squirmed away from him.

She yelped and squealed to get away. "Ugh, gross!"

"Take that!" He snickered and chortled as he shoved a finger full of cum into her mouth.

"Ugh no! Guh…" She wiped her mouth, trying to spit it out.

"Uh oh... kitty gonna spit now?" He snickered again.

She growled at him in warning.

"Meooow," he mocked her then hissed, making as if to claw her face.

She lunged at him and bit at his throat.

"Oh no you don't!" He wrestled her down.

They wrestled a bit together before he took off his shirt and wiped the rest of the cum off both of them. It had dried in places and left them both sticky and crusty.

"Well, so much for that." He threw his shirt down and finally did up his pants.

His scent was all over her, and she was used to it now. She reached up for him and nuzzled his neck, lightly nipping at his skin where she still tasted the residue of his cum. He closed his eyes and lie down with her. "Oh... silly kitty." He ran his fingers through her hair and she sighed contentedly.

After a long moment together he spoke, "You know, we're going to have to get up and shower, don't you?"

She mumbled, "No... let's just sleep here."

"Come on, kitty! Up you get!" He rose up and half dragged her up with him. "We'll play more later. Let's clean up and then... I can show you the new toy I got you." He smiled, pleased with himself.

"Wait, there's more?" She asked incredulously.

"There's always more with me, kitty." He stroked her neck and nipped her throat with his teeth.

She sighed. She was a very lucky kitty, indeed.

MY BELOVED GAVE ME A ROSE

By Sumiko Saulson

When my beloved offered me a rose
It tickled my skin and teased my nose
A study in lovely repose
Blushing skin reddening
Rising heat from within
Heaving chest, heavy breath
Under fingers curled soft petals
Of rising and writhing flesh

Nails upon petals, teeth upon stem
Lips upon chin bitten lower lip
Hand firmly to hip
Resistance all stripped
Heated breath upon neck
Palm firmly besetting rear
Hand against cheek, sweetly
Smacked until roses appear

A rosy blush, adrenaline rush
To tease, to touch, to bruise and crush
To cradle and love, enslaving thus
My love now encased in verse and vase
As warm as a tender embrace

THE LEFTIST APPENDAGE

By Serena Toxicat

"This new survey shows that women dress for each other, not for men. What's sad is that we women don't include ourselves in the women we dress for."

As it dawned on Lyra that she was in for another spat with the emotional baby she called a boyfriend, she started to second-guess her breakup with her girlfriend.

"Are you saying it's better to dress for women than for men? I mean…what are you getting at? Do you think women are more worthy of being catered to?"

"No, Moran, I'm not."

"Stop pronouncing my name moron!"

"I said Moran. Not my fault the two are so close together. I just brought up the survey because it made the news. Most people still assume that women take time shopping and primping to impress men. We don't."

"Everybody's different. I just wanted to make sure we're on the same page with the whole gender thing. I was alienated from the restaurant where I worked because some nineties riot grrls didn't want anybody with a penis around."

"Any gender can have a penis."

"Ha-ha. I know, I'm just saying…"

"What do you mean? The owners fired you because you were a guy? Isn't that illegal?"

"No, I was friends with a lot of the customers. They were mostly people from the music scene. But this girl clique got all into Courtney Love and Bikini Kill and turned into a gang of feminazis. They ordered me to serve them their veggie burgers and soy shakes and shut the fuck up."

"Feminazis?' Wow. I don't mean to be PC, but couldn't you find a better word? I'm sorry that happened, though."

"They told me to stand there and look pretty."

"Well, that is less labor-intensive, at least."

"Har-dee-har. It's not so funny when you live it."

Lyra heard the irony in that male angst and chose to keep her pesky woman-thoughts to herself.

"Well, I won't make you feel less-than because of some silly appendage hanging between your legs," gushed Lyra playfully as she side-hugged her manchild.

"But you're used to dating women. How do I know I'm not just some stinky boy to you? And what do you mean by 'silly appendage?"

"Haven't we already ironed this out? Come here, stinky boy."

Lyra pulled Moran to her on the bed and wrapped her legs around his waist. She stared into the brown of his eyes as they went from triangles back to pools. His voice softened and the aforementioned appendage grew harder, and much less silly.

"What are you going to do to me, Lyre?" he teased.

"I don't know Moran. What were you thinking?"

"I stopped thinking right about the time you started lifting your shirt up."

"My itty-bitties aren't so bad now, are they?"

"Not if you cup them in your hands and feed me."

Lyra held back a puff of amusement. She had barely started dating Moran and had already had it up to her pierced nipples with his criticisms of her barely-Bs. Was Moran not breastfed as a baby? Surely his sticky-like-flypaper mother was more than attentive in that regard. Lyra grabbed her bouncy "riot girls" and poised them close to his pillowy lips.

"Here. Suck them."

Moran licked and flicked as he undid his fly.

"Do you want me to get the clamps?"

He didn't wait for an answer, and the conspicuous appendage sprang to action. He urged Lyra to take it between her breasts (a boobie trap if there ever was one) and moaned as he watched it navigate her cleavage. The 100%-organic moisture created a slip-and-slide that the appendage found to be great fun.

"Oh, Moran, your appen…I mean your, you know, feels so nice there."

"It does. Mmmmm," he moaned, ignoring her near-miss with his penis-labeling, as he pinched each of Lyra's nipples with a metal clamp

Twi, one of Moran's alters, was up in front, cocky, fully associated, and nearly integrated into his host.

"Uhhhhh! Smother me," one of them commanded lustily.

She couldn't be sure who was giving the orders but she was already in a compromised position and didn't much care. It was her cue to move up the host's earthly vessel and grind her velvet riot-pussy in his mouth. His tongue parted her plush curtains and then the threadbare ones, and his lips sucked them in. He honed in on her clit barbell, and his mouth followed the same routine. Male Rights Activist-in-training or not, he liked eating pussy and that was feminist enough for her. She couldn't give him much air or he'd lose momentum. He and Twi did their thing until Lyra came, and they knew her climaxes by her shaking thighs and pleased cries. If some of this was Twi's doing, then she didn't mind the alter hitching a ride.

And if she had had an orgasm, then so should they, right? Fair is fair. She flipped herself around, planted her flushed, wet femme-bomb in his still-willing lips and teased the head of his appended bot with her tongue. She was attempting to stifle a snicker. Maybe a candy-cane move would help her concentration. If he only knew that she was still amused by the whole "appendage" thing, he'd freak out and break the mood—and possibly some mirrors. He and Twi were prone to that.

"Mmmmmm. Keep doing that," he motioned.

She kept up her barber-pole tongue swirls and segued to a rhythmic sucking of his attentive appendick. The more she sucked the more of that thing she was able to take in. The beginning of what she assumed to be some deep-throating signaled a new stage: BJ Intensity Level 2. Moran pushed his rooster higher into her throat, abandoning any interest in her cunt. Who needs that passé pussy with this as an option?

Lyra wished she really did have a clit hiding out in her throat, but knew that there were more useful things to wish for in this relationshit. His pumping grew too enthusiastic for her throat and she drew her teeth gently down his shifting shaft as if to say, "you won't strike oil here."

"I know it's kind of late to mention it," asked Lyra, "but do we have any spiked rubbers?"

"I think so," grunted Moran. "Check the nightstand."

Lyra drew a silvery packet out of the drawer, peeled the wrapper off with her teeth, and slid the latex body bag down his breathing shaft.

"Mmmmm. Sit on my cock."

Lyra mounted that cockrock with her swollen femme fruit and snorted to herself as the words "femme fruit" streamed across the screen in her head. She hoped that the well-exercised appendage would fancy those lips as much as it did the ones on her face.

She never knew with the finicky Moran and his shadowy alter. Doesn't every self-help book say something about communication being key? Maybe those crazy love-cats would have to pick some locks. Lyra had been everything in Moran's head during sex—or everyone, at least—the town 7-11's trashiest teens, his first-grade teacher, Miss Ratto, who looked like Olivia Newton-John in her prime, his little sister, and even this guy he knew. Imagine that—a dude!

With Twi sharing his head, there was double the clusterfuck to consider.

Moran would never admit it but Lyra could tell when his "connection" was down. She had felt herself shift into different girl-thoughtforms (and one guy) as he manifested them. What a wet, hairy, enmeshed mess!

At least his meeker alter, Fin, would be reliably checked out for a spot of tea. Ah, well! Neurotypicals fantasized, too. This was the same deal, basically. Any relationship with The Moran System would be a polyamorous one with those head-squatters. She'd be better off getting with the program and imagining her own sex-people. Things were growing complicated on all fronts. Moran's lupine alter began growling and snarling at seemingly random moments. Whatever the things that haunted him were, they made themselves known with nary a hint of modesty. What lived in Moran and what tore through him became an entangled nest of mindfucks.

One night, when he and Lyra embarked on a binge of his suicide threats, her tears, and their angry emoting, an etheric specimen of astral wildlife breezed past. This was no alter. Lyra supposed aloud that it was a ghost dog, but both she and Moran knew better.

Neither could tell if the sensation of malevolence they both sensed came from the eerie critter or from their fear of it. Moran told Lyra that tomorrow was another day, and they tried to calm the chatter in their heads just long enough for the distractions of the light to take over.

Upon awakening, he reached for the nearest phallic object to feed Lyra's pussy.

"Bet you didn't expect me!"

It was Twi.

"You're the one who wants a dildo in you first thing in the morning, not me, and you know it. Scram!"

"Me scram?! That's parts discrimination!"

"No, it's not. It's amputating an appendage that has needed to disappear for a very, very long time."

"If I go, I'm taking Moran, Fin, and the entire system with me!"

What really sucked, badly, for Lyra, is that Fin was Moran's most delightful part. It hurt to envision him a collateral casualty.

"No way, Twi the Twat."

Lyra left Twi there to bug Moran. Something wet streamed down her cheeks. The thought of her partner leaving was almost unbearable. Almost.

Twi had gone into the headspace to pick on Fin, leaving Moran at the helm. The host--her partner, her lover--was back in control.

PERSEPHONE'S PLEA

By Francesca Gentille

I do not seek to have a Master
I seek to have a King

I do not seek to submit
I seek to give a vow of sacred service

I do not seek to submit to one who is above me
I seek to surrender to one who is beside me

I do not seek a collar
I seek to be crowned

I do not seek to be trained
I seek to be guided

I do not seek to be a slave
I seek to serve my Lord

I do not seek to be dominated with power
I seek to be ravished with love

I do not seek a Dungeon of Bright Pain
I seek a Temple of Dark Eros

I do not seek to lose myself in the heights of pleasure
I seek to find my soul with Hades and Persephone in the Great Below

All I seek
I am prepared to give

I am waiting
The Lady in her tower
Waiting here

Not to be taken
but to be won

ANDONA'S FEAST

By Sumiko Saulson

Shadows, embracing primordial forms, clung to the naked figures on the bare grass in the forest clearing. The townspeople were preparing Andona's gifts for the Harpy's Feast. The first of them, a strapping and healthy young lad named Mandid, was ready. He clasped the bottom rung of the rope ladder and climbed up into the tree to Andona.

Andona crouched in the darkness, tendrils of smoke encircling her taut breasts, long black wings extended below the branch upon which she sat. Below her toes gripped the tree's bark with razor-sharp talons. Her wings were tipped with finger-like appendages, each of these graced with sheer, raking claws. She was the last of the harpies, the rarest of treasures in all of Naminiton. Andona was eager to feed her multiple hungers.

"I am here for your pleasure," the young human offered, wrapping his arms around her neck. His legs straddled the branch below her. His erect penis was tightly bound in rough twine around the base to keep it painfully swollen and rock hard for her pleasure. He moved a hand to his mouth, moistening two fingers between his plump plum lips before slipping them into her folds. He fingered her gently until she was moist, excited. Then, he slid his cock deep inside her. Grinning, she wrapped her wings around his back and sunk sharp talons into her lover's yielding flesh. He reached behind her and began to bind his ankles together, so that his legs were restrained, encircling her ass.

"The first gift of your feast is offered, bound for your pleasure" he whimpered, placing his arms around her neck once more. Once both hands were in place, he grabbed a noose at the opposite end of a length of twine handcuffs binding his left wrist, and slipped it around his right.

He pulled them taut around his wrists, holding them in place around her neck so that he might stay put when she ascended in flight. The harpy cawed, and then leaning over his neck, snapped long, sharp canines into the vulnerable human flesh. She licked and sucked his blood while rising aloft into the sky.

"Eat!" the townspeople cried out in unison. "Devour what is yours, Andona!"

She rose above the crowd to display him nude under her wingspan, his deliciously muscular buttocks thrusting with all of its might as her fangs gouged deep into one side of his throat. This continued for some time.

Then, the ropes began to unwind! He kept his arms and legs clasped together as long as possible, clinging to Andona long after the bindings fell lose. The villagers stared at them, waiting to see if she would bring him to ground or let him drop from high above, breaking his neck.

Satisfied with his performance, the harpy descended to a ceremonial rock outcropping called the Offering Stone below. She lay him down upon the Offering Stone, and hovered over him as he continued to perform his sexual duties. She bucked in excitement, talons digging deep into the flesh of his shoulders. Blood gushed from open wounds and trickled down the rough-hewn stone in rivulets, like a waterfall. When she came, he came too… as if compelled. She tossed his tired, spent body over the side of the Offering Stone for the villagers to collect.

The young man tumbled down a hundred feet and hit the floor below. Hands reached out to help him stand up. Bruised but not broken, Mandid stumbled off with two of his brothers, who were proudly clapping him on the back. "You made it out of her alive, Mandid!" the older brother shouted approvingly. Andona cared not a whit that the young man was living. She returned to her branch to wait while Foti the Priestess prepared the next sacrifice.

Foti, a statuesque and ancient human woman with walnut skin and rose-red hair assembled in a messy nest atop her long, lean head, led the ceremonial preparations for the feast. The Priestess was topless, each of her nipples were pierced through with a curved piece of animal bone in the shape of a tiger's fang. Her bare navel was embedded with rubies. A translucent skirt of fine silk encircled her otherwise bare thighs and naked pubis. Seashells adorned the belts around her waist.

A group of nubile young women ran with little to no clothing and carefree through the trees. They appeared in the clearing, baskets of fresh fruits atop their heads, or plates of dried dates, cheeses and meats in their hands. They quickly assembled them on a series of low stone tables for the feast.

"Prepare yourself and be a worthy gift to Andona!" The Priestess Foti called out to the living gifts, which were standing in a line before her. She would examine each in turn before selecting the next offering.

Foti ordered the nearest of the tender supplicants to present his willing flesh to be made ready for the Harpy's Feast. She handed the youngling faun a bucket of honeyed milk and a half dozen pea-sized balls of scented soap. He grinned happily upon receiving the items, and made a brief traditional speech offering himself as a gift to Andona. Foti then moved on to the next supplicant, a delightfully pert and busty female gnome of indeterminate age. The living gifts were quite varied in appearance, but all were here for one reason alone, to please Andona.

"I have chosen," she said at last, pointing a crooked finger at the next gift.

"I am ready!" a young female elf cried out from the furthest end line. "I am prepared for my supplications."

"Watch and learn," Foti ordered the crowd, approaching the girl. She looked her up and down, fondling her soft, blue skin pinching her taut azure nipples, and smacking her across her round little blueberry ass cheek. At last, she smiled.

"This one is the honored effigy of the Priestess Foti," the wizened one grinned. The girl gasped, holding her hands to her cheeks in excitement. The pleasure at being chosen soon gave way to nervousness. Several men standing near her nodded approvingly. "Her plump little breasts are perfect for the feast," one of them remarked salaciously.

"Do your offer your perfect young bosom willingly to suffer in my stead?" Foti asked her. "To be pierced as I am pierced, and to be thus raised in agony and offered to Andona?"

She lowered her head obediently. "I am Lok. My breasts are an offering to Andona in the place of Foti, and it is my honor to endure all of the rituals Foti once survived in her stead and to suffer as she did."

Practically drooling, four of the men grabbed her by her arms and legs, holding her still for the preparations.

"My agony was exquisite and wonderful." Foti assured her, slipping two fingers between the warm, damp flesh of Lok's vulva. "So wet! So eager!" Foti announced, showing her glistening fingers to the crowd. "How the thought of your punishment excites you, lovely one."

The elf blushed and trembled.

The four men carried the young elf to the middle of the field, where the others gathered around to observe her public chastisement. They used metal shackles to bind her wrists and ankles spread-eagle to the ground. The tallest of the men handed Foti a pair of fang-shaped bones, each three inches in length and about an eight inch in diameter. The villagers uttered incantations as Foti leaned over to pierce the skin just below Lok's right nipple with the first of the bones.

Lok's piercing cry attracted Andona who flew over to investigate. Agitated, excited, the harpy extended her exceedingly long and narrow tongue and licked the red blood dripping down the side of Lok's blue breast. The elf moaned and writhed as the tongue slipped around the nipple and the outcropping of bone. Foti quickly pierced the other nipple while the two of them were distracted.

Each of the four men slid a leather thong into a hole in one end of one of the bone piercings. Once all four leather strips were attached, they grabbed the free ends and bound them tightly to Andona's ankles. The townspeople applauded as they ran at Andona now, frightening the harpy until she lifted off into flight.

"Make her bleed for you, Andona!" one of the villagers cried, as the harpy soared into the air, pulling the leather thongs tight with her ankles. The girl's breasts were pulled up with her – stretched to the limits. The girl's back arched to give more slack to the bindings.

Foti laughed and leaned over to pinch the straining nipple. "Take the pain as you were meant to, and be pleasing to Andona."

Suddenly Mandid, the first of the offerings, reappeared in the clearing. He chuckled at the spectacle before him. "Foti sure is the sadistic one," he observed.

Foti cackled. "Indeed, I am!" she admitted. "Unbuckle her restraints."

The four men bent down and unbuckled the elf's shackles and began to chase the harpy with sticks until she began to drag the girl along behind her. Lok pushed herself up by her palms and stood on her feet, running after the alarmed harpy while she attempted to take flight.

That was when the first of the bone piercings snapped in two, loosening the elf from a bond, but not freeing her entirely. The harpy dragged her along by her remaining thong.

"Pull it out with your free hands, idiot!" one of Mandid's brothers cried out, laughing as Foti cracked the girl across the rear with a solid bamboo stick. A red welt appeared on Lok's behind. Dazed and confused, the girl began to fiddle with the bone stick and the leather thongs that held it in her chest, desperately trying to unbind them as she ran after Andona.

"Don't listen to him," Mandid screamed. "Just snap the bone in two!"

"Madness!" the brother countered. "It's too strong to break, and if it did, that'd hurt like hell." Mandid ran after Lok and grabbed her by the back of her heel, laughing as the harpy Andona flew overhead, pulling the little elf like a piece of bait. Lok bounced up and down, her breast pulled taut by its thong. Andona batted her wings, unable to escape.

"Come back and taste!" Foti beckoned to the harpy, casting a bedazzlement spell with her twisted wormwood wand. A pallid green haze formed around Andona's face, and a look of lust came over her eyes. Bewitched, she changed her trajectory downward. Pressing the talons of her toes deep into the elf's skin, she clutched a breast in each foot. First, she shoved her down into the dirt, and then she launched herself up into the air, carrying the dangling blue form below.

Mandid was forced to loosen his grip.

"There it goes!" yelled the excited crowd. Long sticks swatted the back of Lok's knees and bottom of her feet as the harpy dragged her over to the offering stone. Mandid clambered upon the stone where he'd lain with the harpy earlier.

One of the men above, standing on the outcropping, used a sharp ceremonial dagger to carve a line in the shape of a serpent from his left pectoral through his shoulder blade up to his ear, and called out, "Drink what is yours, Andona!" Smelling his blood, the harpy turned to run into him and tore into the side of his neck with the force of her sheer hunger. A gaping wound gushed blood between his hapless fingers.

"My blood for Andona!" he cried, laughing as he held his hand tight against the wound.

"It is an honor to bleed for her!" Foti cried. "How I suffered for her!" She lifted her elongated breasts to show the young man the scars below, from when Andona had carried her aloft just like Lok. He smiled wanly as his vision began to dim due to blood loss. Then, he toppled to the ground, hitting his head and opening a gash at its side while he fell off the platform.

"May you survive it!" Mandid called down to him, finally arriving atop the plateau.

"May you prove yourself worthy!" the man cried back, before falling unconscious.

"Take and mount her!" Foti called after Mandid. "Take her before Andona!"

Mandid nodded, and pulling a curved knife from his belt, sliced through the leather thong that held Lok. Then he placed his hands on the elf's shoulders and pulled her closer to his flesh as he lay back against the rock. Slathering his rigid cock in a paste of coconut butter and the blood of the fallen, he pressed the head of it towards the elf's buttocks.

"Mount me before Andona," she whispered breathlessly, thrusting her hips on to his impaling rod. He obliged, wrapping his arms around her chest, one below and the other above her breasts, so he could keep the harpy from lifting her off again.

"Observe the feast of Andona!" Foti cried, running around the rock in a maddened circle, dancing as the sun descended and the moon began to rise.

"Eat what is yours!" the crowd roared. Obediently, Andona loosened her claws, and beset upon the presented offering with her teeth. Sharp fangs buried into the elf's neck, sucking her blood. The long, snake-like tongue flickered over the wounds in her chest, licking and suckling upon swollen breasts. Finally, Andona's mouth clamped over Lok's rising mound of Venus, sucking and biting while the human, Mandid, took the elf from behind.

"All is madness during the feast of Andona!" Foti cried. Around her, the villagers began to fall upon each other – sex upon sex, mouth to breast or genital or ass, grinding in a writhing mass of lust as the show proceeded above. Wine was sipped, fruit eaten, and lustful appetites sated below as Mandid and Lok offered the feast to Andona above.

REMOTE CONTROL

By Lydia LaRue

You set the task and I eagerly obeyed, however there was one catch —

I had to do it all with composure while you held the remote control to the vibrating ball inside me.

You stood there with a smirk on your face, daring me to disobey while you had me crawl on all fours to where you were.

Buzz

I felt the sharp vibration inside me and paused, but you beckoned me onward, impatiently tapping your foot for effect.

I crawled to where you stood, laying my head on your foot as you gave me a pat.

"Good girl," you crooned. "Now fetch your leash." You pointed to the closet room where your bag was stored. and I had to remain on all fours, never quite knowing when you'd press that button.

"Don't make me wait," You warned, watching me through the wooden bar slats, making sure I remained on all fours. But it was really hard to unzip your bag with my teeth, and you must've seen the frown on my face because you came over then.

"Oh, no. Naughty girl… I'm going to have to punish you later for that." You unzipped the bag, found the leash and held it before me, silently ordering to grab it within my mouth, and I did. You made me crawl out first and then I felt it —

Buzz

Buzz!

I gasped, holding the leash in my teeth, and trying not to drool.

You stood before me once more, and then gently took the leash from my mouth. and I waited as you put the leash around my neck and then proceeded to lead me around.

"Oh no, wait!" I thought with trepidation as you led me to the social area, for everyone to watch and stare at me. My head was down in embarrassment. and I didn't look up as I heard a few comments. But you said nothing and quickly led me back to the play area, back onto the rug.

I was very vulnerable in this position, dressed only in my black lace underwear and nothing else.

"I am his now, I mustn't resist." I had arranged this play scene after all.

"Look at me." You ordered and then —

Buzz

I felt the vibration inside me and from my kneeling position it seemed to vibrate along the folds of my flesh to my clit and I couldn't help but let a moan escape me.

From your pocket you took a cloth and dropped it on the ground then said, "Polish my boots. Make them nice and shiny."

I quickly obeyed, now allowed to use my hands though I crouched low to the ground as I buffed and rubbed your black combat boots. but I should have known what you would do…

Buzz* *buzz* *buzz!

I felt it as if through my legs and my thighs shook a bit as my hand fumbled for the cloth again.

"Naughty, naughty. Did you drop the cloth?" You bent down in front of me and I could see a slight bulge in your pants as you were enjoying this, degrading me and teasing me just enough to make this scene really hot.

You grabbed my hair, hard enough for control but not too hard to bring pain, and I softly sighed a whimper.

"Ah, ah ah… that's a no-no." You tutted and mocked, me then pressed the button.

BuzzzZZ!

I tried to pull away from your grip but it was useless as you held me by my hair then took a tighter hold of the leash, wrapping it around your hand a few times while with your other hand you still held the remote control.

Slowly you stood up, and I had no choice but to raise myself, onto my knees as the leash pulled on my collar. But this brought me facing the bulge in your pants and I kissed it through the cloth.

"Bad girl, you know better than to tempt me." You joked but I could see the flush of your face and your hardened erection. "Pick up the cloth."

I obeyed once more and you took the cloth from me, shoving it into your pocket with the hand holding the remote —

Buzz

"Whoops, did I do that?" You grinned wickedly and I couldn't tell if you did that by mistake or on purpose (most likely on purpose). Then you led me by the leash, onto all fours, before you stood behind me.

"Get that pretty ass up in the air. I'm going to give you your punishment now." You looped the leash onto your wrist with your hand still on the buzzer and I could guess what was coming next.

Smack

On my right buttock then —

Smack

On my left.

You kept hitting me…

Smack!* *Smack!* *Smack!* *Smack!

Until all of my rear end was throbbing with the resulting impact and probably very red by now.

And then —

Buzz

Smack!* *Smack!

Buzzz* *Buzz!

Smack!

Each in alternating patterns until I lost track of what would come next. All I could do was moan and whimper on the floor until I felt like losing all control.

But I should have known it wasn't over. More humiliation would come next.

You came around to face me, taking off the leash and putting it into my mouth before you ordered, "Don't you dare cum yet. I'm going to get something. *Stay!*"

I was left on all fours, waiting on the carpet with the leash in my mouth that tasted like leather before I felt it.

Buzz* *Buzzzz

And then

Buzzzzzzzzz!

It was as if you had your finger pressed on the button and wouldn't let go. Unless it was stuck?

I desperately struggled and moaned, trying not to let my body lose control, but it was sooo hard!

Finally, the buzzing stopped and I looked up with blurry eyes, out of breath, to see you standing before me with a plastic dish in your hand. At first I thought you were going to make me eat out of it or drink water but you didn't put it down yet.

Reaching for the leash from my mouth, you led me then to a far corner of the room then crouched in front of me and I saw the lovely view of your erection through your pants directly in front of my face.

You put the plastic dish down then got up and moved behind me and started to slip my underwear off. The bullet vibrator was still lodged inside of me.

I wondered what you would do to me as you pulled on the leash for me to move, right over the plastic dish before you said, "You're going to do as I say, because I'm your Master."

You held the remote control with your other hand. "I order you to cum into your dish."

WHAT?

No way. Is he really going to make me —?

But it was too late. You pressed the button and didn't stop.

_Buuuzzz_ZZZZZZZZZZZZZ

I gasped and moaned, in a low guttural tone and my body seized up in an uncontrollable spasm. I came, HARD.

It was humiliating and degrading.

After I orgasmed, I bent down to cradle my head on my arm. But then I felt the vibrator inside me slip out, into the plastic dish.

Oh no…

"Oh Yeah! Good Girl!" You groaned with pleasure as if it had been you who orgasmed and then you said, "That was so good. Now lick it up."

I raised my head. Did I just hear what I thought I heard?

You turned the remote control off, slipping it into your pocket, before you grabbed my hair and whispered into my ear, "Lick it up, Baby. Lick it all up."

You stared into my eyes and I knew you were serious and for a moment I had second thoughts but I could hear your panting breath in my ear and the grip in my hair became a caress along my neck as you gently pushed me down to my dish.

I started to lick at the vibrator ball in the dish, tasting what had been inside me moments before, now sour and wet as it clung to my tongue. You avidly watched me and with your other hand, started to stroke at your erection within your pants.

I finished as much as I could before I looked up at you pleadingly. You grinned and moved the plastic dish aside before you caressed me lovingly then surprised me with a kiss on my lips.

I put my hand on your erection as you undid my collar and leash, taking it off of me. I nuzzled into your pants, placing my lips onto the cloth that held you restrained then I undid your pants and freed your member from within.

You sat down on the chair nearby then took out the condom you had in your pocket all along.

"Put it on," I ordered and you laughed.

"Hey, I'm the Master here." But you opened the condom and put it on.

Your penis was the perfect size for me, not too big or thick, as I eagerly took it in my mouth, holding the base of it with my hand as you leaned back in ecstasy. I sucked, mouthed and flicked my tongue over your penis while I enjoyed your reaction of pure pleasure.

Even with the condom on, you were very sensitive and I luxuriated in providing you this release and worked without hurry to bring you to your climax.

Your hips bucked slightly and I worked your body into a rhythm with my mouth, always on you, as my hands caressed the base of your penis.

Minutes had already passed but I didn't care how long it took, only that in this moment, your pleasure was my only concern.

You gasped and moaned, occasionally raising your body and arching your back as you came closer and closer to the end.

I took you as far as I could down my throat and moaned, almost on the verge of choking myself which gave you a thrill as you watched and finally let loose.

You moaned and gasped, "Oh Yeah! Yes!" Closing your eyes in absolute submission to the climax, you leaned back breathing hard and helpless as I carefully pulled the condom off you, placing into the plastic dish after tying it.

"The Dish of Cum," I thought with amusement.

Your hands reached for me and I laid my head on your knee as you caressed me. After a short while you re-did your pants, and I gathered my underwear, putting them on again.

You bent toward me and gave me another kiss then slowly got up and gathered the leash while I picked up the dish, holding it before me as if in offering and you laughed.

"Behold The Dish of Cum," I joked and you burst out laughing, putting an arm around my waist as we walked back to the closet and I put away the 'sacred dish' in the one of the plastic bags I carried in my purse.

I put on my purple satin blouse and dealt with cleaning the area we had our scene in before we both made our way to aftercare to sit together and cuddle. It had definitely been an intense scene and one I wouldn't forget soon.

"Thank you, Master." I said, only half-jokingly, as I nuzzled into your neck.

"Your wish is my command." You answered softly.

"Hey, that's my line!" I laughed and you kissed me on my nose.

From then on we talked and joked, you with your shiny boots and me with my satisfied body, until the aftercare was over and we went to join others in the social area.

I blushed, remembering how you led me in front of everyone but most of them were in their own scenes now. We relaxed, ate some food and drank some drinks until it was time for the club to close and for us to go home.

"So, what have you got in mind for next time?" You asked as you got into my car.

"Oh, you'll see. I have to go home and write down my ideas first." I grinned mischievously.

"Are you going to write about this?" You laughed and I nodded.

"Of course. I am a writer after all and this'll make a great story."

I drove you home, eagerly awaiting the time when I could get home to put all this down as my mind reeled out more exotic scenes for next time.

LETTER FOUND IN THE WRECK
of a Pirate Ship Sunk in the Caribbean
April 10, 1947

by Kaleidoscope Eyes

an assemblage derived from Pablo Neruda's poetry

Body of woman, white hills, white thighs, about your ocean eyes:

It's as if those eyes of yours had flown away from you, and as if I can write the saddest verses tonight, verses which could hold their sound just off the metal of my pen. Just one thing surrounds me, a single motion; I feel the same missing thirst and the same cold fever adding up to the same messy and miserable sums as those moving the old ship over the old waters. All of a sudden I seek permanence in time and limits on earth like pure sound, a sound like dreams or branches or the rain come to shock a notary with a cut lily.

Between dull explosions of brimstone and reflective waters, my feet weighed down with a red fatigue, with all the signs of life, among the beds. Above all, fingers at my throat–

Raúl, do you remember? We fought in the most genital terrestrial territory, with no earth, no abyss, and at dawn, barely uprooted from your Andean foam, we scraped away at the womb until we touched man: Juan Coldeater, son of the green star.

The ancient lamps, the lashing whips around common graves received me when you received yourself, Raúl. All of our strength returns to its beginning.

Body of woman, white hills, white thighs, about your delicious body:

Your whole body holds your falling book. I heard wine-taunts flowing over your glistening flesh and over unfortunate public tigers: two bodies overcome by one honey. I love you without knowing how, or when, or from where.

The raucous rivers of the ocean flood set out the settlements and arrived.

Body of woman, white hills, white thighs, about your hidden blood:

One single being, but there's no blood that has passed since I last saw him. He came from, from winter or a river, in this net in which not just the strings count but also my blood, which I scarcely ever saw coming in and out of the market that lives among the foam. Behind him, behind that market, lies despairing love, and there never was a choice between you and Juan, Raúl.

Invincible and alone, keep hoping, Raúl, that autumn will arrive to introduce us once more.

CAN WE TAKE TURNS? SWITCH WITH ME?

By Francesca Gentille

Don't be my 24/7 submissive
Being in charge of you full time is tiring

Don't be my 24/7 Dominant
Being guided by you full time is repressive

Dance me with in the flow
of shifting energies & Inner Personalities

Now I am in charge
Now you are

Now I am on top
Now you are

Now we are floating, melding,
merging, converging

And no one is in charge
Except perhaps The Divine

Meet me in Primal Power
Let's test one another's claws
And both surrender to passion

Be my God sometimes

so I may worship at your feet
And adore you from head to toe
inside and out
darkness and light
Allow me to be your Goddess sometimes
so I may experience your knelt worship
And adoration within and without
And feathered kisses of energetic reverence
darkness and light

Be my mirror

By my opposite

Be my potential

Remind me of my past

Help me envision a radiant future

Meet me in vulnerability

Let us heal one another
in places we long to go
and have never been

Switch with me

A NEW SENSATION

By Lydia LaRue

He lie back on the bed but kept his eyes open. He wanted to watch her. This would be something entirely different.

She washed his feet first. It was too simple a term for the immeasurably luxurious feeling she introduced him to. Never had he ever had his feet bathed before. The softest brush scrubbed him and she massaged his muscles and tendons. He felt so relaxed he could hardly imagine her doing anything more to put him at ease. With a heated towel, she dried him and got him ready.

What she did next would stay in his mind long after their encounter together.

She was naked as she requested. He enjoyed her nude body though it didn't do anything for him physically. It was about service and devotion.

"I want to serve at your feet," she whispered to him.

He delighted in her eagerness.

She showed him pleasure he never imagined he could have.

Her hands grasped his feet and she placed the soles of his feet on her breasts. He wiggled his toes on her and she giggled. He tried to grasp her nipples with his toes but failed. It was a strange thing to do but he laughed too. Then she scooted down and bent to brush her hair along the top of his feet. Her hair tickled him and a few strands ran between his toes. He felt a slight stirring in his groin but ignored it. He didn't want any distractions.

She began to kiss the top of his feet and then the inside of his arches, ankles and heels.

He moaned involuntarily and was shocked at himself. He hadn't known he would enjoy this so much.

She brushed her lips up and down the soles of his feet. That did it...

he moaned louder.

He was watching her mouth his toes before she took his pinky toe in her mouth--her hot breath teasing him and making goosebumps all over his body. Her wet lips slipped over his skin before she took the other toe in her mouth, not touching her tongue on him yet. She repeated this with each toe, in and out, in and out before moving to the next one--a preview of what was to come.

It was quite exquisite.

He felt himself getting harder and didn't quite know why. Normally he was never aroused by anything sexual and yet... this was completely new to him.

“Are you all right?” she asked and he nodded.

She smiled and was enjoying this. “I like to watch your reaction. It's very... thrilling.” she said softly.

He nodded again, beyond words.

Her hands slid over the top of his feet and he shuddered.

Then she began using her tongue.

She started toward his heel then ran the width of her tongue up to lap up the tip of his toes.

He closed his eyes at that and threw his head back in ecstasy.

She was giving him a tongue bath and it was the most erotic thing he ever felt... mostly because it was forbidden. He had his earlobe licked, his neck licked, his chest and nipples licked--even his dick. But this was so... dirty. Feet belonged on the ground not in someone's mouth.

And yet it felt so good.

He started to whimper. That's the only expression he could find for the repeated whining in his throat as she thoroughly licked in swirling patterns all along the soles of his feet. And then the underside of his toes... then in-between... then she sucked on his big toe... and each toe after that on the left... and then the right.

He was just about thrashing on the bed, running his hands through his hair and down his chest. He was only semi-hard but wasn't close to an erection. He had no need for it. Chills ran through his body and the hair on his arms rose up. His nipples were hard and he brushed them through his shirt.

He lost himself in the sensation.

Pure ecstasy.

He felt himself come down at last from the euphoric high.

She looked at him and he beckoned her up to him.

He held her, wrapping his arms tight around her as she nuzzled into him.

“I have never experienced anything like that before. It felt... so good.” He sighed and shook his head. He lifted her chin up for a kiss.

"Thank you for that. It was amazing."

She kissed him back. "You're welcome, darling."

They both closed their eyes and settled in for a long nap together.

The floating sensation of bliss followed him into his dreams.

THE PICNIC TABLE

By Ouroboros Sings

On her back, strapped down spread-eagle, and surrounded by chaos:
A sharp elbow digging into her chest
The wicked tendrils of a flogger slapping her breasts
Biting clothespins sinking into her tender flesh
Vampire gloves pawing at her inner thighs
And a cold steel dildo sneaks into her pussy

A face leans in close
A smiling face that fills her field of vision
A face of such beauty and serenity that it holds her
Mesmerized

"Breathe in…"
She breathes in

"Now exhale…"
She exhales
A hand grips her neck and clutches tight

"One…"
The sharp elbow digs into her ribcage

"Two…"
The wicked tendrils grow more stingy upon her breasts

"Three…"
The biting clothespins now gnash her labia

"Four…"

The vampire gloves drag across her belly

"Five…"
The cold steel dildo begins to pound her pussy

Stars appear
The gripping hand loosens
Oxygen fills her lungs and returns her to the chaos

"Very good—now breathe in…"
She breathes in

"Now exhale…"
She exhales
The hand again clenches around her neck

"One…"
The sharp elbow twists into her bicep

"Two…"
The wicked tendrils slam down on her thighs

"Three…"
A hand yanks the biting clothespins off her labia
"GODDAMMIT!"

"Four…"
The vampire gloves squeeze her breasts

"Five…"
The cold steel dildo won't stop pounding her pussy

Stars appear
Her body writhes and arcs as she screams and cums

The hand lets go
The chaos calms
Oxygen fills her lungs and returns her to the present
The looming face gives her a gentle kiss
And smiles

TRANSLUCENT SKIN

By Sumiko Saulson

"You will find it near the coral reef at low-tide," Naedra's father had told her. "Find and fetch the amphibiod home. Only encircle it about the waist with a slender chain of wrought iron first, which you will find at the fence. That will prevent it from using any of its magic against you."

"It is wrong to bind an amphibiod," her mother had warned. "Ignore your father's instruction, child! It is the way of men to use force, when you could use seduction. Seduce it instead, with tender kisses, so it might grow enamored and follow you willingly."

"You endanger our daughter without cause!" Padre howled and cussed at Madre as Naedra slipped out the back door. Opening her leather pouch as she tip-toed past the fence, she quietly piled the chain into her bag. Better safe, she felt, than sorry.

She continued on her quest, until she found the ambipiod leaning against the coral reef at low-tide at the crack of dawn. It lounged against the rocks, long mane of ruby-red fins decorating its pretty head like the fans of a Betta fish. Its skin was translucent pearlescent silver, and below one could see clearly the function of its heart, liver, lungs and intestines. Even its reproductive organs were transparent like a fish of some sort. Opaque testes and ovaries coexisted in the scrotal pouch below its tailfin, as the creature like all its ilk was intersex. Its wide-set frog-like eyes protruded slightly, each red with a rectangular black pupil.

"You've come to steal my magic," it said without emotion, but a rapid blinking of its eyes and nervous licking of lips betrayed its fear.

"Why steal what you will give me willingly?" Naedra asked teasingly, running her finger over her bottom lip, licking it, and then biting. The creature squinted in what she wasn't sure whether to interpret as lust or cringing in response. It rubbed its thighs together nervously.

"Many a young maiden yearns for the seed of Pinadoia," the ambipiod bragged. "It pretty things desire. It longs to believe that the pretty things are in awe and lust over its beauty. How well do it know better. The human only wants its semen for her witchery crafting, to cast spells and make potions with."

"Then give me your seed," the girl demanded, forward and confident. She began to strip down, allowing the creature to take in her firm, brown bosom… bare, chocolate skin tipped with brandy-wine colored nipples her lovers assured her tasted sweeter than the ripest of plums. She dropped her pale white blouse into the ocean water, where it drifted languidly to shore. Her tiny black shorts, removed, were stuffed into the leather pouch adorning her hip.

"Upon my lap then ye climb," Pinadoia huffed nervously, offering both its hands to her. Each hand had upon it three long, webbed fingers with bulbous tips, and no opposable thumb. Rather than climbing its lap, Naedra took one finger into her mouth, sucking it suggestively. It was important to establish who was in charge of this exchange.

Much to her relief, Pinadoia grinned. "What be your name then, human wench?" it asked, winking.

Carefully removing its finger from her mouth, she answered, "My name is Naedra. Allow me but to entice you and you will become mine, not just today but for always." With that, she took both hands and ascended its lap. Her hand gently guided its wet finger inside of her labial folds. She lay against its chest, rocking back and forth against it, moaning.

Overcome with desire, Pinadoia clutched Naedra's breast with its remaining hand, all three fingers stroking the inch-long dark nipple. Pinching it gently, then tenderly releasing, it fondled the tight round orb of her breast with delicate fingers. Soon, the tendrils between its thighs began to elongate.

"Allow me to release you," Naedra purred, climbing off its lap and into the water below. She found it's long, tentacle-like genital strands waving in the sea. Each of the three arms of its pudenda looked like an octopus leg but free of suckers, when not erect. Now, all three stood at attention. She groped and stroked them the way she milked the cow's teat at home until it was ready to spill. Then, she pulled a small mason jar from her pouch, and captured its jizz in the container.

Locking the jar, she slipped it in her pouch, and turned casually to walk towards the shore.

"Wait!" Pinadoia cried out behind her. "Aren't you going to imprison and bind me with the wrought iron shackles in your pouch?" it asked.

"Why would I do that?" Naedra responded. "It is not right to bind an ambipiod who is unwilling. You are free!"

"Well I don't want to stay here and give my seed to just any old human pretty that comes by wanting it!" Pinadoia protested, leaving the coral reef to follow her to the shore. "You said you would keep me, and so you must keep me! Be true to your word, human!"

"Very well, then," Naedra grinned, handing the chains to the amphibiod.

"Should I place the binding upon my waist?" It asked, gleefully. "Shall I call you mistress?"

"Just carry it for now," she replied calmly. "Yes, you may call me mistress, my pet."

"Your pet is a good pet," it purred, carrying them dutifully in its arms all the way back to the farm.

"Padre, this is my pet, Pinadoia," she told her father, prancing proudly out back, to where her parents kept their containment pool.

Her Madre, smiling, followed her out the back, waving to Padre as she sassily strode pass him. "I told you so, Padre!"

"Stick to your own pet!" Padre barked after her. "Don't touch Naedra's. I wish you would both keep them chained. It makes me nervous, how it does as it pleases when it isn't serving you."

"He's so jealous!" Naedra giggled, taking her mother's hand as they danced outside to the beautiful saltwater pool. It featured a waterfall at the back, and a small coral reef at its center. An ethereal being with lucent skin; long, bright yellow gills, tendrils of orange and gold lounged, fanning itself with a seashell.

"Come meet Naedra's new friend, Omandu!" Madre called out to the creature.

"To see is to want," Omandu purred, blushing as peach as the coral below it. Pinadoia swam out to the reef and offered itself to Omandu…

"If it pleases mistress," Pinadoia asked.

"Of course, beautiful one," Naedra nodded. "I have never seen such a thing. It would be my delight."

Tentacles winding one against the other, mouth suckling mouth, skin pressed against see-through skin. Mother and daughter held hands as the two slid tendrils in and out of orifices, fingers pressing soft and vulnerable erogenous spots. And as the twinning two reached the crescendo of orgasm, Omandu discretely shifted a sliding container ensconced into the islet below them to capture the oozing ectoplasmic cum the amphibiods produced.

"Lovely!" Madre cheered, clapping. "What a joy it is to watch two beauties performing for our pleasure and their own."

Omandu slipped down off the coral and carried the semen to its mistress, Madre. She nodded and smiled as she received a glass jar with seashell lid, embracing and kissing her pet. Pinadoia followed sheepishly behind, setting itself on the floor at Naedra's feet, where she gently ruffled its head.

"It is wrong to bind an amphibiod," Madre said wisely. "Although a witch wants a familiar for her spells, it must be seduced, and not forced into servitude."

"Indeed," Naedra agreed. "One must not take by force a thing that must be given freely."

"It spoils the magic anyway," Madre said with a wink.

ADUALITY {0≠2;1=108}

By Seruus Ualerium Tristissima Liber

An excerpt from a work in progress

She's saved my life dozens of times with it by now, but that Association-damned giggle of the captain's still grates on me. It's not even the sound of it so much anymore, but the immediate image that flicks its way across my brain, the conditioned response. I'm not even looking at her at the moment, and I can see her wide-blinking pink eyes, devoid of concentrated furrow context, finger twiddling bright blonde hair. At least her great-grandmother had chosen an interesting eye color for her genetic strain to carry.

"You'll just have to refuse the job, Captain Ulysses."

I'm sure that I'm showing the strain of keeping my voice unirritated in my hands, posture and fidgeting feet, but it's the tone of my voice that matters.

The lights glare and whine in a slight crescendo, warning me that the effort is costing me. I pull up a diagnostic in my AR; nothing about their current, luminosity, or functioning has changed in the last twenty minutes. It's confirmed, then. I sigh, just to convince my muscles to relax.

"Dove can't power the Electrical Messiah with me in eir condition, and I'm supposed to attend the Union Tent on Franklin Prime to get trained in emergency solo operations a month from now. As in the future, as in I'ven't yet."

I watch the ripple of facial changes spreading from that statement.

Shit. I bet those are looks of disapproval; I must have mouthed off to the captain again. Luckily, she herself is oblivious, as always. I wince as the light becomes distracting, and my back curls seed-like as my abs try to pull me into myself. I need to go, now.

"Your face just went flat," speaks First Officer Grippe, absent-mindedly flipping green-and-purple hair back over zir head while bent over the sewing that kept zem busy during these meetings, "and I see those muscles working, Awiti. Problem is we think this job comes from the Company."

A hush claims the dining table of our tiny little semi-criminal starship, the entire crew quiet for once. The Company kept plans within plans, and never let even the smallest risk to humanity stand for long. Rumors claimed that they offer their jobs to very specific crews for very specific reasons, and that to refuse them is to be a risk to humanity.

The problem was thinking only moderately. If your crew never thought deeply about their jobs, where they came from, and what they meant, then the Company's black-jumpsuited agents would have no problem making sure that you would do what they wanted you to do. On the other hand, if the meaning of your jobs was a constant riddle probed by a deep-thinking crew, they'd be able to identify the faint clues that indicated that they had less choice than they thought, and would be able to decide to save their lives. It was only those who thought enough to question but not enough to notice what they see who were in danger.

My overwhelm building; I couldn't modulate my volume very well. "But we've only a single Unionist, and I'm useless alone!" Great. Now Ship's Ecologist Brazil is backing away from me, taking refuge in the door frame vacated by its barrier with a soft woosh. He doesn't really do well with loudness; ironic, really, considering the rough-weave-clad man had fled a planet clanging with constant advertisement.

A giggle ~ *that giggle* ~ answered like an unseasonal summer rain, quiet slipping its way into sleeping dust. "Like, I can totally do it."

Noöpilot Paramhamsa was still new to the crew at the time. He's still insufferable to this day. Bending slightly from the bottom of his rib cage, he loosed his creakily refined voice: "Christmasing yourself demoted, then, Cap?"

A raspberry blown from a young mouth answered his retort, eliciting an indulgent chuckle from the trench coated queen of a man. It came from a small girl whose pink eyes, thin and floating atop impossibly high cheekbones, power-clashed quite nicely with the hummingbird colors of her hair, shock of red bright against rainbow-glinting green.

"You wouldn't have a ship to fly if it wasn't for my mom!"

"That, you're true, Doll." He knelt to look Doll in the eyes, his upper body never changing shape. "That you're for certain true, small friend."

I began to flex my hand, hard fist to splayed star of fingers trying to escape each other to dawn-smoked umber skin stretched bone over knuckles to as big a circle as my five fingertips could spread and back again, repeating in simple rhythm, rhythm slower than my breath. My brain had sunk into the tendons and cartilage of my phalanges, so I almost missed First Officer Grippe's comment. "No, wait, that actually could work."

"Jaomai: how?" demanded New Mary Desiderry, slick and polished despite the industrial mess that clung to him occupationally, hair agleam with constant brushing. "She's not a Unionist! I love her, but she's a glorified ideal of a slave-wife who managed to wiggle free of her planet's patriarchy despite them trying to kill her for it, not a Unionist trained by the guild to raise and direct orgone in conversation with the Spirit Association of Benevolence!"

"But that self-same patriarchy had a vested interest in making sure she knew how to fuck well, Seligman—"

"It was, like, the only schooling," Captain Ulysses interrupted herself with another of those incessant giggles, "I was, like, allowed."

"Exactly, my sweetly beloved cunt. And that schooling included techniques derived from those the Guild teaches. I've seen both standard Unionist practices and what Toy does myself, up close and personal, and there is indeed a lot of crossover."

Ome-Mazatli-Miquiztli, Esquire, asked through a mouth of tortilla wrapped around spicy honey-candied cactus (her favorite dessert), "We're talking five days here, though. The guild spends a lot of money and effort heavily modifying Unionists' bodies for endurance, stamina, ability to produce and maintain high levels of sex hormones and neurotransmitters for extended periods, responsiveness, and many more qualities in order to allow them to do this work."

"Ummmm, like, I don't know what all that means," another giggle, this time with a bounce, "but, like, my ances . . . umm, ansis . . . like, my mom's mom's moms made sure that we would, like, always be ready to serve however we were meant to. My name is, ummmm, Toy, so I was, like, sposeta be used as a toy. For fucking. So it's, ummm, kinda like what they do to Unionists, I guess?"

"Why are you looking at me to confirm?" First Officer Grippe asked the crew. "Toy knows her own body as well as you do, genetically engineered brain or no. What do you think, Awiti? Can you make it work with your captain as your partner?"

A diaphragmatic sigh rocked my body. "Do we ever have a choice? I guess I'll have to try."

"Like, yay!" A torrent of giggles glittered poundingly on my ears, complete with bouncing - at least her petite clapping was rhythmic. "You're, like, dismissed. Do what you, like, need to do to, like, calm your body down, okay? And then, like, figure out what we need to do. Meeting, like, totally over."

She stood there, twirling her hair, blinking over-large eyes at the copper and zinc machine which seemed stark against the matte persimmon of the brushed metal wall behind it. I knew the feeling. I remembered with typically perfect accuracy the first time I met the machine, which sat unfazed across the room from Captain Toy Ulysses, survivor and instigator of the Lover's

Quarrel, doomed to the freedom she desired. Its waist stretched out like the four elegant corners of a large table, the only languorously simple bit of the New Motive Power, the Electric Messiah. The legs beneath angled in with a slight bulging curve and were meticulously scrolled with writhing bodies, gender and even species getting lost somewhere amid their quiet frenzy, giving metal the appearance of warm and salty flesh.

An outline of a rectangle like a hexagon pulled upwards, formed by two metallic rods rising until they were connected at the top by a revolving steel shaft which supported a crosswise arm of harsh steel, reached up from the table surface. Two large square bottomed pyramids of epoxy resin and metal shavings contained magnets and dangled from this arm's two extremes. Under each was that very curiously constructed fixture which so casually fascinates the eye, a sort of shallow oval bowl, formed of a peculiar layering of magnets, wood, and metals, filled with water, and above that a number of zinc and copper plates, alternately arranged; the two served as organic and electric reservoirs, respectively. These were supplied with lofty metallic attractors that reached gracefully upward. As with most ships, various metallic bars, plates, wires, magnets, insulating substances, peculiar chemical compounds, etc., adorned our Electric Messiah according to the doting arcane nuances of our New Mary's incessant tinkering. At certain points around the circumference of these structures, and connected with the center, more pyramids hung alternating with small, steel, magnet-enclosing balls. A balloon structure hanging between the table legs inhaled and respired gently, like the chest of a sleeping lover, growing to delicious size and then lazily draining air into the rest of the machine.

I felt myself begin to be aroused, blood rushing to my cheeks and sensitive bits, the invisible shift as my cardigan accommodated tightening breasts and assertive nipples, the muscles of my hips and legs loosening. My dress worried me, as my trinket pressed against it, ruining the line of its fall past my hips; I no longer felt the hem along the front of my thigh. I wiggled my toes ~ a ritual of sensuous anticipation ~ and a giggle interrupted my enjoyment of the precision with which this ship part was made.

"Ummmm, okay, so how do we start?"

"I usually start with a moment of appreciation of the well-made machine we'll be powering, Captain. Gets me in the mood, as it were. That being said, I suppose it's time to engage with you."

She pranced closer, steps too quick for me to track, and suddenly all I could feel was the sticky slipperiness of her latex, pink with her considerable features offered with pale blue outlines, as our closeness pressed its bulges against me in ways both random and predictable.

My hand somehow found itself swimming through her blonde hair, so wavy and full it might have had froth. "And then like what?" Her breath smelled of flowers and the musky moist dirt from which they grew.

A tightening found itself in my fingers, gripping her head from the back and dropping, inch by inch. Her knees bent and, upon the slightest caress of the floor, splayed. More smells accompanied quiet moans as her excitement left the psychological behind and exuded from her body. I managed eye contact as I reached over to press the button letting Noöpilot Paramhamsa know that he could start telling his steering story.

Now it was my turn to break the moment, as that notification called all the usual readouts and graphs to crowd the negative space around my captain in my AR. I blinked them away with a shake of my head, unable to deal with that much information in such an unfamiliar mindspace, and whatever had come over me, that selfsame mental state I had hoped to protect, dissipated.

Panic. A racing to the brain neurons that seemed too heavy to move, paradoxical metaphor. The lights hummed and the floor flashed. I was aware of each cell of my skin and its unique experience of clothing and of an oddly comfortable giggling. My muscles wanted to move but had forgotten the six directions.

Cold air sharp on my trinket followed by the scratchy soft of a tongue creeping up its length. The point of a chin poking the pillowed organ beneath it. There was no envelopment in this, no gulping or pulling, just a calling out (giggled vibrato pressed up against my pelvis sending heavy pressure through all my joints) to which I rose. A shuddering breath pushed my eyes open with the feeble strength of the wisps of muscles clinging to my ribs, rather than the force of my lungs.

Captain Ulysses sat back on her heels, meticulously maintained nails steadying me and maybe herself against the backs of my knees. My trinket peeked as if from genital curiosity from beneath the soft cloth that once had hid it. She waited, patient, permissive, unable to even comprehend that something might be wrong.

Maybe her ancestral gene tampering wasn't such a cruelty as the rest of us thought.

I squatted, taking her hands from my knees to my shoulders. Unready for eye contact to resume, I let her lips take my full attention. Plump and shining with gloss, they seemed to have more in common with overstuffed vinyl cushions than flesh. She was plastic and she was free.

My own brain turning itself off, my lips tugging the rest of my body forward, mashing against hers with unprecedented fervor, tongue darting out and then hiding back in its toothed pocket. I gave myself over to hormone-driven momentum and jackknifed my legs open, right hand grabbing my captain by the throat and the left stretching vanguard to catch the wall I was propelling us toward. The length of her body was pressed between the stretch of mine and that persimmon-colored metal that squeaked beneath my fingers as I buried my mouth in hers. Certain of the sustainability of our verticality, I slipped my left hand to the bubble of her butt. Just below, actually, to the unclad spot where the muscle of the thigh shrugs off the fat of the ass, but the feel of flesh felt wrong. A couple of inches upward and plastic pleased. I gripped and kneaded and needed and the small husky cords among my vocals began to plead in words that were not quite gasps and not quite moans.

Captain Ulysses' arm brushed mine as she lifted hers to point, pulling my mouth behind my eyes and off of hers. A slight pulsatory and vibratory motion could be seen in the pendants around the periphery of the Electric Messiah. "That just means it's working, Captain. We're doing a good job."

"We are?"

"Yes. You're a good girl." This was met with a happy giggle that invited me to mentally run through all the sociological information about Kore's Retreat. Eager to be a reason for her to feel pleasure, I sought culturally appropriate ways to raise the orgone. "Well, maybe ~ what makes a good girl?" A crinkling of the brow, a slight fear in the eyes resonating with the flutter in my chest. Against all odds, we were syncing, without struggle or awkwardness. My study worked!

"Doing what I'm told?"

I threw her into the pillowed pit in the center of the room, fuchsia and ruby cushions swallowing her like candy still in the shiny wrapper. "Get up." She did, and I was shocked at the grace. "And?"

"Ummmm….Always being on display?"

"Press that blue button on the wall next to you."

She complied, twittering as feet floated off the floor.

"And?"

"Like, being dumb?"

The bottom half of my face transmogrified into an unfamiliar smile. Plush fabric bubbles began to fall upwards like slow-moving sakura. Captain Ulysses' feet began to drift apart in the absence of gravity and floor's friction, making a wishbone of her legs and rolling her skirt into a belt. Well, more of one. "Right! That's a good girl, which you most certainly are."

I wish I'd sounded more like I believed it, but blame it on the queasiness the suddenness of zero-gee always brought on. Once again, she had no idea anything was wrong. Biologically-enforced no-mind was a wonderful thing. Wet glistening provided matching contrast to latex shine as she slowly revolved her waist an axel. My mouth watered and I dove.

She tasted rich ~ spiced must and good olive oil, complete with that masochistic burning freshness at the back of the throat. Jammy, silky, and oaked, I drank her like a fine wine. Like an eager dog drinking fine wine, that is ~ I used my nose as much as my lapping tongue, wagging my head back and forth to flick her clitoris with its tip and distort the words I was writing upon her lower lips in overlapping salivary letters.

We spun slowly, lost in these complexities until she convulsed with a gasp, slicing her body folded. My ears became handles as she slathered her body with my flesh, squeezing arms and legs around my body to stop my emergence where she wanted me. I thrust my pelvis back to change our momentum and then breath exploded from me as we bounced against the ceiling. I heard her moan.

A seed-like curl brought her steaming wetness dragging along the length of my trinket, sending sensory overload blazing through my body. I wondered if she'd studied like I had or had an AR HUD giving her predictive heuristics like I did ~ somehow she knew not to fill herself with my trinket, that this raised my orgone but insertion would ground the ship as there'd be no way to power the Electric Messiah after that. But she couldn't even read: her brain never grew the specific neuronal pattern to process visual information that way.

Leaning back, Captain Ulysses used one hand to plop her large breasts over the top of her neckline, struggling against her dress's tightness to make them all the more available. Her heart-shaped nipples were a vibrant red painted beneath her pale skin. This moment of breath allowed me the time to process the fact that my overwhelm had passed by. I brought my HUD back and checked where we were in the orgonic generation process, and how that matched up to Noöpilot Paramhamsa's progress in attaching our von Neumann hook to the Casey Jones Effect. Crap. We were about to miss the simultaneity point. This needed to get fixed fast.

I grabbed Captain Ulysses' ass and hurled up with all my strength, spinning her again, this time quickly, like the flywheel on an engine, carrying myself around as well. Hands on the floor arrested my motion and with as much speed as I could achieve I scuttled backwards to where I knew she would be. An oof brought her fingernails scraping across my now-bare belly. Ah, there it was, sweetly aggressive growl lurking in my throat, "Take me, Captain."

Toy shoved my hips straight down, flapping one arm out to hit that blue button. Gravity emptied my breath in one firm pound and my breasts jiggled from the impact of her fingers, firm flutter finding each hidden parcel of nerves, scraping firm nipples. My trinket strained with rhythmic blows that squeezed it between our bodies, growing harder and more tender with each beat. Teeth like panicked butterfly wings nibbled my windpipe like she could swallow all my polysyllabic words, make my speech simpler and hers more complex, like this union of bodies could make communication possible between what too often seemed like our two species.

Like this family of a crew could finally cure each other's loneliness.

Her ministrations twisted my spine into an arch that didn't know whether it was going to the left or right and screwed my eyes so tightly shut that new landscapes of light burst against the blackness of their constriction. My mouth could only open in a soundless forever gasp, a guppy-shocked inhalation that leaked whimpers across the eggplant-colored floor. It felt too good, it seemed, like the lightning that flashed across my neurons was going to light my serotonin on fire, ignite my oxytocin, flash-electrolyze all my dopamine in an explosion of thoughts dissolved into flesh.

Suddenly, everything ceased. Cool, dry air caressed my skin rather than moist warmth. Cautiously, I opened my eyes after a moment passed, just in time to see that Captain Ulysses had discovered the toy rack in the wall. Finger cutely tapping chin, she gyrated up and down to investigate her options, lingered on each toy that caught her eye while I made a game of running my fingers up and down my trinket in the same exploratory motions as hers.

That was when the shift happened, the moment when the starship and everything in it is transmuted by the noetic drive, twisted from physical space into storyspace. As we'd both witnessed many times, the other person grew more individual and self-defined, distilled into a unique archetype that felt somehow symbolic of large groups of people. We became two communities fucking in intertwined narrative styles, Freytag's pyramid inserting itself into kishoutenketsu, syuzhet dilating its ring structure so nivolas can enter.

Our journey, always the same five days in length from our perspective, had begun.

FOUR HAIKU

By Ouroboros Sings

Taking Sir's great cock

'Tween his parted lips, he said,

"Mmf fwmph bmph mmf *cough *"

+

Writ upon her breast

His wet, cumly signature

Contains a typo

+

Fuck me in the ass!

No—*you* fuck me in the ass!

Stop being an ass!

+

Her red, throbbing clit

Glistened under candlelight—

Dammit, no condoms

FIRESIDE LEGENDS

By Lif

I graze one talon around Erim's breast, starting from beneath, and curving around up to her collarbone. Enough pressure to leave a faint white line in its wake, which quickly reddens. I then lightly trail it up her neck, directly along a vein that I take great care not to damage or puncture. She does not break eye contact, gazing straight into my eyes in total trust, as her hand continues its work between my legs. Her rhythm does not break, or even waver. Just like her mind.

Not so long ago, this human girl tried to sacrifice her own life just to kill me. She was ready and willing to die, all just to end me, and to save her best friend. In her mind, she had accepted her own demise as the price of my defeat, and all to save her friend who had gone off in search of me out of her own self-damning curiosity. Much as I mock the self-assurity and arrogance of humans; and their delusions that they might defeat me, I could not help but be impressed with her. Of course to be fair, it had partly been my own carelessness; as well.

When her precious friend Rothka had entered the Stone Forest two days ago, I allowed my own sexual appetite to consume my focus and I lowered my awareness. I was careless. It was not every day that a stunningly beautiful, rosy-cheeked, red-maned young woman came trespassing into my front yard. I had first noticed her even before she entered the maze of stone columns that was my home. She hid in the woods that lay outside my home, no doubt gathering the nerve to come closer. I was perched on a rock formation near the top of one of the columns. My skin was carefully matched to the color of the stone, and I was careful not to move. Soon, she stepped out of the trees, and fully into the moonlight. What a sight she was!

Rothka, as she would later tell me her name was, had a pale skin that stood out in sharp contrast against the stone, particularly in the moonlight.

She had a small frame, clear even through her coat. With every other step, I could catch a glance of her legs. They were slim, with no extra fat, but clearly not regularly exercised; either. I was impressed that she had made it this far in the wild on her own. Her hands were quite telling too: they were among the most delicate I had seen in a good while. No calluses and no scars. She had led a life of innocence, and it showed - not just in her skin, but the naiveté of a girl such as her standing in full view of the Stone Forest, alone, in the dead of night. She was taking in the sight of it all (as best she could with such nearsighted, human eyes) without any regard as to just how visible and vulnerable she was; in turn.

When she inevitably stepped close enough to the stones, I began channeling the mists around her, and as she began inhaling my intoxicants, there was no resistance. I had encountered the type; before. She had come here specifically because of the stories. She was mostly certain that it was all a mess of tall tales, but under the surface, she secretly wished it could be true. That said, it was only a matter of moments before she could feel herself becoming aroused, with no visible stimulus. Her hands were on her coat and squeezing before she was even fully aware of it. When she heard my whispers reverberating in between the stones, just as the legends would have said, her eyes went wide, not with fear, but joy. She was lost to me within moments, listening to my murmurs within her head nurturing desires that matched my own. The moment I stepped into her view, her only emotion was awe. She beheld me, my majesty, and fell to her knees as though she had been graced with the presence of a God...which, in her mind, was precisely what I was.

In their legends, they call me a demon. Of those who have found me, most came to call me a god. Frankly, either word suits me just fine. One has little difference from the other; each is a figment of mankind's imagination, a greater being than themselves with powers that are not at all dissimilar from my own. As such, who am I to deny them their mythologies and fireside legends? Such stories inspire fear, respect, and even a healthy curiosity, which is precisely what leads to meetings such as this.

That moment was short-lived, however, before an arrow struck my left wing and shook me entirely from my work. Though it was certainly painful and bleeding for now, the wound was nothing serious. The webbing of my wing would grow back and heal over. The real damage was that I would not be able to fly for several days, which was exactly my assailant's plan. I had been so caught off-guard, it was almost embarrassing. I had not even enough time to gather fire before the girl I had not seen or heard coming body-slammed me, wrapping her arms around me as she used her momentum to propel us towards the ledge in clear hopes to send us both to our deaths. Naturally it was useless in the end, but impressive even so.

Rothka watched, still dazed and unable to make her own decisions as far as what to do. When I told her to remain still and not move she was visibly relieved to have the decision made for her. Erim, the new girl, was enraged at the sight, spitting curses at me for what I had done to her friend, and suddenly her own motivations became clear. This was a rescue attempt.

I took Erim's wrists in mine before she could reach for the knife that hung at her belt. She moved to kick me, but I had already exhaled a deep breath into her face before her boot struck me, and she had breathed in before she realized what was happening. She stumbled back, her face flushing and her breaths coming heavier. Realizing what I had done, she screamed, leaping back from me, but the work had begun. Humans are delightfully carnal creatures, and they rely far too much on indulgences to be able to resist my natures for long. All I do is bring to the surface what's already there and let the rest become background noise. For Erim, I could already see her hands beginning to shake with desire, her skin beginning to shine with sweat, and her chest straining against the leather of her vest.

It took her over an hour before she finally succumbed to my powers. I could have easily ended it sooner of course, but I was far too fascinated by her will to resist. I much more enjoyed letting it burn down like a candle, as her lust built. Even after she had begun to pleasure herself, even after she had shed all clothing, she shook herself free of the stupor three separate times. The first time, she again tried to attack me. The second, she simply hurled more insults and profanity. The third time? She begged, at last, for all of several minutes before finally giving in.

The last two days have since seen the three of us quite occupied. Indeed, I think that I have taken a particular liking to Erim, more so than most of my encounters. As lovely as Rothka is, with her blood red mane and cream skin, Erim is infinitely more captivating, but not for her delicious tan skin, or her toned arms and legs. Not for the way she chewed her lips in determination that night. Not for her brown eyes, or the hair that was one shade lighter than black, tied behind her head, begging to be pulled free. Not for every freckle or subtle imperfection on her tanned skin that reminded one how very alive she was. Not even for her breasts, which are admittedly perfect, standing high and proud almost any way that she stands, or for just how many options her flexible muscles offer me.

No. Erim is beautiful for her incomparable spirit. That burning heart, filled with courage and willpower like no human I have ever broken or tasted before. And now, as she kneels between my legs, steadying herself against my thigh with one hand as her other strokes me with perfect rhythm, I have had the sweetest of victories. One could argue that I have not erased her entirely, per se. As I cup her face in my claws, each point resting in her flesh so that the slightest twitch could ruin her face at best, and kill her at worst, it is clear that one thing has not changed - she is still willing to die for me, in her devotion. The devotion has simply been repositioned. The bravest and most determined of her tribe is now my most devoted thrall. She is no less powerful, no weaker for being my servant. Rather, all of her strength is now in my employ, precisely where it belongs.

As she repositions, a drop of her wetness falls to the stone beneath us. Noticing where I am looking, she looks down, and back up at me in silent question. I give a single nod, and she smiles gratefully, reaching between her legs, gathering her wetness on her hand, and slathering it on my member. Before she resumes her stroking, I pull her hand up some, by the wrist, and lean down to taste her juices off her little finger. I savor the tang of my devotee on my tongue as she continues to pump me towards the edge. She leans forward to take me into her mouth for a moment and as she slowly pulls back, sucking in with all of her wind, her tongue moves expertly across the underside of my shaft.

I have held back climax long enough, and am almost ready to let myself come on my newest favorite. So captivated am I by her that I almost forgot poor Rothka where she lies on my bed, pleasuring herself to the sight of her would-be rescuer servicing their Lord. She gasps when she sees my member twitch, and I remember her. I watch her finger as it moves in circles between her legs, her wetness mixing with her sweat, her body heaving as she gasps, and the sight is enough to finally bring me to finish, the first jet of my seed hitting Erim straight on her cheek. The second lands directly in her mouth, and the third on her breasts. Throughout it all, the warrior proudly leans forward, eager to use her entire body to catch every drop in display of what she is - mine.

I watch her gathering my fluid with her fingers, bringing them to her lips without breaking eye contact for a moment, proudly sucking each drop down loudly in presentation for me, and I smile - in approval of her work now, and in anticipation of her task tomorrow. After all, the tribe will be missing their warrior and her friend, by now, and Rothka does have a sister…..

SPIT AND PATHOS

By Sumiko Saulson

I dreamed I had all the right words
To tell the story of you and I
Running right in like we hadn't got sense
When we were new and free and wild
And nothing we did could ever be wrong
When we first began crafting our song

When everything was playful and sweet
With breezy hearts and light feet
Dancing beat to beat step to step
Silhouettes in darkened rooms
Opening ourselves to everyone
In places where you come undone

But maybe we opened gifts too fastly
You classy, sassy and pretty but lastly
Nervously stepping out into the light
Waiting for everything to be perfectly right
What a lovely package to undo
All of those bows and ribbons containing you

Not a painting or a picture to be held still
In motion like life itself, doting images

Or chivalric love, a muse that fit me
Hand in glove, but what is it to love
A muse, and what tools does an artist use
To hold you still in my mind's eye?

Low light and dark walls can't contain
You lovely as a study of sunset in oils
But besoiled and besmirched and unfolding
In secret places, eyes closed, mouth sealed
A rebellion of butterflies cascade from lips
Covered in a thin glaze of spit and pathos

How I could not be moved by your plight?
Constrained by shackles of your own
No hand truly your master but your own
I'd take your side just to come along and see
You ultimately free, destiny in your hands
Because wild things shouldn't live in cages
That they don't own and operate

THE TRIP TO THE ABANDONED FACTORY

By Lydia LaRue

Everything was going according to plan.

I drove to the abandoned factory by the railroad tracks, not quite believing that I had you here beside me, holding all the goodies we got at the porn shop. At the shop they had lots of rope, so we bought enough for our scene along with a flogger, riding crop, latex gloves and condoms with lots of lube.

I wanted to be prepared as much as possible and I had a sleeping bag with the plastic tarp in the back of the car trunk. It was too good to be true. Everything I mentioned to you, you were willing to try. I never thought I'd find anyone as adventurous as I. But here you were: young, cute and oh-so-willing, as I abducted you, taking you to a place you've never been before, to a place beyond your wildest dreams. You were mine now, to do with as I pleased.

"Do you still want to do this?" I asked as I parked the car behind the tracks, near the orchard trees where hardly anyone comes by.

The place was deserted and the abandoned factory rose up from the field in a derelict display of horror where monstrous things waited within.

"Yeah, let's do this." You agreed so easily.

We got out, I grabbed the tarp and sleeping bag from the trunk, and we made our way to the factory, climbing under the broken chain fence which did nothing to keep the meth-heads and transients out.

"If we see anybody, we'll go." I said, knowing that the place was sometimes patrolled by the owners who drove around the lot. As luck would have it, nobody was around and we had the whole abandoned building to ourselves.

Graffitied walls loomed before us, announcing unearthly arrivals of creatures from the nightmarish corners of drug-addled minds.

"Got the scissors?" I asked and you pulled the safety sheers from your back pocket and nodded. "Good let's begin."

I chose a spot in the building under the tall metal rafters that stood the test of time, weathered only by the bird poop and bat guano from above. I laid the plastic tarp down then the sleeping bag over it. In the corner a few steps away lay the time-neglected machine, used long ago as part of the factory that made matchsticks. Tiny, shrill squeaks of rats (or maybe bats) chirped from it.

You looked around; taking the scene in then undid the rope after placing the flogger, riding crop and black bag containing: gloves, condoms and lube, within reach on the sleeping bag.

"Are you going to take your clothes off?" You asked and I shook my head.

"I want you to take them off." I smiled as you eagerly obliged, undoing the buttons on my shirt before pulling it off then reaching for my shirt underneath to pull it over my head.

"You wear a lot of clothes." You laughed before taking off the final spaghetti-strap undershirt I wore instead of a bra.

Your hands went to the button of my jeans as you leaned in close to me. I took advantage and kissed your full, beautiful lips, stroking your long hair and the strong jawline of your handsome boyish face. With one hand you reached in-between my legs, stroking me over my underwear while I slipped my pants down. We kissed some more as you stroked me and I know I was getting very wet for you. I held onto your shoulders while I stepped out of my jeans and you bent down to help me with my shoes and socks.

I did a little strip-tease, just for fun, as I took off my underwear and held them dangling over your crouched body before you snatched them away with a flourish and I laughed.

Now I was completely undressed, with my clothes laid together on the sleeping bag. You ran your hand over my breasts as I ran my fingers through your hair, kissing you as I pleased and lingering over the features of your face. You held me close and I could feel the hardness of your penis through your pants, where I rubbed you, enjoying the sensation I felt as your penis twitched in pleasure before you sighed.

"I'm ready now." I said and you smiled and laughed, grabbing the rope.

"Ah, what should I do first?" You asked playfully. "I think I want you on all fours."

I slowly bent down, hands and knees upon the ground, raising my buttocks in the air slightly. I have to admit, this put me in the most vulnerable position, not only awaiting the moment you would tie me up, but being here in this place was possibly one of the most dangerous things I've ever done. I'm not sure if this thought was going through your mind but you didn't seem fazed by this activity, though I kept my ears aware of any outside sounds for intruders or patrol.

You started with my legs first, tying a double column tie and securing my legs together tightly, making sure I had enough circulation. Then you tied rope around my waist before you said,

"All the way on the ground, lie down with your legs up. I'm going to hog-tie you."

I could hear you were enjoying this and I could picture your face smiling, all lit up in excitement while you ordered me into position, making me entirely helpless to your skill and will. I lie with my chin resting on my crossed arms in front of me, until you reached over and ordered,

"Now your hands behind your back."

"You're making me totally immobile, aren't you?" I joked.

"That's the point." You answered smartly.

I could feel the taught pull of the tie you made as my hands were tied behind me to the rope at my waist and to my feet. I tried to glance behind me but I couldn't twist all the way. I saw you make several knots into the rope to finish it off.

"There, now you're totally helpless." You smacked my ass playfully and I felt a sudden panic coming on.

I am a bit claustrophobic and putting myself in this situation was a mistake but I wanted to prove I could do it, that I was capable of pushing my own boundaries. We had gone over the safewords: *"Red"* for stop, *"Yellow"* for check-in and *"Green"* for go — yet there was still the possibility that you wouldn't listen to me, which you could still rape me.

I started to sweat and I felt the droplets run down from my armpits. You grabbed the rope flogger at my side and came around to face me, bending down to stroke my hair and I was grateful for the attention.

"You look so good tied up like that." You spoke softly.

I smirked as best as I could with my chin on the sleeping bag.

"You ready?" You asked and I nodded and smiled.

You looked around cautiously before beginning and I liked that you kept yourself aware of the surroundings, since anything could happen while we were distracted by our play together and it would not be a good idea if some creep came up without warning.

The coast was clear and you began, raising the flogger up before I felt the dull smack of rope against the bare skin of my ass.

I groaned in pleasure, free to shout or scream as I pleased since there was no one around for a mile to hear us and as the train ran by, it drowned out the surrounding sounds.

Thud. Smack.

You alternated using the flogger and your bare hand, before you gripped my ass roughly in your fingers. I felt the faint breeze upon my buttocks as the rope flogger swished through the air to land again on my flesh.

I also felt the blood rushing to the skin there, wondering if I would have bruises later. I bruise easily and did not like the idea of getting them but I had to allow some margin of risk for my pleasure. If worse came to worse, I'd put ice on it later but for now I was enjoying the sensation as you moved the flogger to up my shoulders and back down to my ass again.

You switched sides, to get at one end and the other, since my hands in the hog-tie position blocked the obvious open position for flogging. Then you switched to the crop and I felt a sharp stinging sensation on my buttocks and thighs.

Smack. Smack. Smack — quick flicks of your wrists sent the crop hitting smartly on my body. Harder now you began to hit as I struggled slightly in my rope bonds. You wrenched me back to position, putting your leg over me to hold me still though it really wasn't necessary; it gave us both a thrill.

I groaned louder as you hit harder but then I heard a noise. "Stop — what was that?"

I turned to the noise as we both listened and after a moment I heard it again, then a flutter of wings. It was only a bird upon the rafters dropping a nut (or its waste) on the ground.

I laughed and you rubbed my buttocks gently.

"Can you undo my legs?" I asked, feeling a cramp in my knees.

"Yeah, sure." You loosened the knots and undid the tie, so I could put my legs down, though I was still bound. "Better?" You checked in with me.

"Yes, but I'm still tied up…" I smiled and you did too.

You put the riding crop down and crawled over my prone body, bending down to nip at my neck and ears.

You pressed your groin down onto my red, still-stinging ass and asked, "You said you liked anal?"

"If it's done right." I replied, "With lots of lube and if you go slowly…"

"You also liked your hair pulled?" You asked as you took a handful of my hair in your hand, tugging slowly.

"Gently." I coached.

"I'll be gentle." You reassured me and with your hand reached around my neck. "You want me to dominate you?"

"Yes." I answered. I could feel both your hands on me strongly, one in my hair and one around my neck, as I started to get wet. I closed my eyes, enjoying this new experience. I could also feel the hardened bulge of your penis as it pressed into me while you crouched over my ass.

You bent down to whisper in my ear. "I want to ride you hard. Do you want me to ride you?" Your husky voice, full of lust, sent a shiver down my back and I could feel your breath coming quicker.

"Yes." I answered and you tightened your hold around neck and gripped my hair harder.

"Yes, what?"

"Yes, Master." I couldn't help but smile, hearing myself speak these words but you were pleased.

"Good girl." I heard the rustle of the black bag the gloves, condoms and lube was in.

"What are you doing?" I asked, unable to turn my head around without getting a crick in my neck.

"That's for me to know and you to find out." You answered cryptically then I heard the snap of the latex gloves and the click of the lube cap before I felt the cold, wet touch of your lubed glove reaching between my bound legs.

"Ah, it's cold!" I laughed and squirmed but you held me firmly by my buttocks with your other hand and stroked until I felt your finger go through my vaginal opening.

Palm downwards, you pushed your finger in until you found my sensitive spot, toward the pelvic bone, where I could feel the delicious pressure building. I moaned loudly and undulated my body with the pleasure as you continued to stroke, moving your finger in and out, pressing down to the pelvic bone each time.

"More." I moaned.

"Not yet." You answered, taking your finger out. You undid the rope on my back which held my feet connected to the waist and my hands that were tied behind me. "Turn over." You ordered and I shimmied over to comply.

Now I was on my back, lying on my hands as I watched you take another scouting look around to make sure the coast was clear; it was. You pushed my legs up; loosening the rope just enough so I could spread my legs apart before you knotted them up again. I saw you kept the safety sheers by your side on the sleeping bag and I felt relieved. I was still safe and now you put on another glove and lubed that one up as well before I felt the cold wetness again, this time on my anus.

"Uh, careful…" I warned as you tried to push your finger in.

"Go slower?" You seemed unsure.

"Stroke the outside a bit, warm me up, make me excited." I moved my body to your sensuous touch and sure enough it felt so good that I wanted more. "Add more lube then try again." I said breathlessly.

More cold wetness before your finger finally slid in; all the way. I bucked my hips as you moved your finger, pressing up, with your finger in a beckoning position. I closed my eyes in near bliss as your gloved finger moved in and out of my anus.

"I wonder if I can make you cum this way…" You watched me, fascinated that I would enjoy this so much.

"Yes." I breathed.

You slipped your other gloved hand, with a finger into my vagina,

"I can feel my other finger inside you." You marveled and laughed.

Now two of your gloved hands were working me, fingers going inside, with only my clitoris untouched. My hands were under me so I was unable to satisfy this one desire.

"Please," I begged. "Put your mouth between my legs…" I closed my eyes and moved my body to the throbbing pulse of pleasure your fingers were bringing me--though it was nothing compared to what came next.

A hot, wet sensation met my clit and my eyes flew open to see you bent over, licking my clit slowly.

"Oh, yes!" I moaned. I couldn't keep my body still as my hips jerked up to meet your mouth.

Your fingers moved faster as your tongue flickered and licked.

"I'm going to cum…" I whimpered.

Then your mouth pressed down harder as if to swallow all of me, before you pressed your lips and grasped my flesh, sucking my clit hard. The moment stretched into timelessness as my climax reached its peak. I shouted — no, screamed — my release into the emptiness of the building with only the flight of birds and your grunt of satisfaction as my witness.

I felt an aching in my flesh as you pulled both fingers out, from my anus and my vagina. I weakly opened my eyes and watched as you carefully pulled off the gloves, rolling them into each other, and put them in the black plastic bag.

"Could you untie me, please?" I asked drowsily, still in an orgasmic daze.

You smiled and obliged my request and I gratefully stretched out my sore arms before I reached to kiss your lovely lips, tasting my own fluid and juices upon them.

"Did you like that?" You asked in a low voice.

"Hmm, yes." I replied but you took my hair in your hand and pulled,

"Yes, what?"

"Yes, Master." I corrected myself and you smiled in satisfaction.

"Ready for more?" You stroked my neck.

"What did you have in mind?" I coyly asked.

"I want to tie you up again; flog, whip and spank you some more and then…" Here you smiled mischievously, yet didn't finish your sentence.

"What, Master?" I smiled.

"I want you to suck my dick." You bluntly replied.

I nodded and you took my hands, tying the rope around them, and gently pushed me down on all fours to wait as you picked up the riding crop. Then pulling me up on my knees, you held the rope connected to my wrists and hands and stepped behind me before I felt the sharp, stinging sensation of the crop.

Smack. Smack. Smack — on my buttocks, down my thighs and up to my shoulders. You paused a moment to grip my hair in your hand before whispering in my ear,

"I'm going to make you mine. I'll possess you, dominate you — and there's nothing you can do about it."

"Yes, Master." I answered.

"I could rape you right now and nobody would know…" You placed your hand around my neck, firmly but not too hard as I closed my eyes and breathed a sigh through my tingling lips.

You bent down to whisper in my ear, "You're all mine," before you suddenly bit my neck — hard. I moaned and shied away but you took the rope holding my hands and reined me in, then smacked my ass hard. I struggled in vain to get away but you held the rope firmly and with your other hand, grabbed the rope still tied to my waist, to pull me back.

"No!" I whimpered.

"You're not getting away from me." You snickered and spanked my ass again in reprimand at my attempted escape. "Now for the flogger —" You grabbed it and swiftly whipped it down my thighs and backside again. "Ooh, you're getting nice and red."

I could feel the burning sensation in my legs as the blood rushed to the hot points of impact, while your warm hand stroked my sore skin. Then you trailed your nails down my thigh and I couldn't help but utter a moan at the touch. You held the rope that bound my arms tightly in your hand, while with the other you lightly brushed the flogger along my legs, making me tingle all over as I sighed aloud, voicing my pleasure to you.

I felt the rope holding my arms tighten for a moment as you bent down behind me and then I felt you lick my ass cheek before clamping your teeth on me.

"Ow!" I yelped and struggled helplessly but you held me firmly with both hands on the rope holding my arms and waist.

Finally, I felt your teeth let go of my flesh and heard you say, "Hmm, that's going to leave a mark."

You reached over, grabbing for the black bag and I heard the crinkly rustle of plastic then the dull rattle of condoms in the box. I also heard the frustrated sigh as you tried to open the plastic covering it. I laughed, unable to help myself and you gave me a hard smack on my ass in reprimand.

"Ouch!" I laughed again.

"Hey, quiet!" You ordered but I could hear the laughter in your voice before I heard the snap of scissors, as you used them to open the box. I could almost see your every move in my mind: the unwrapping of the condom, the snap of the lube cap and then listened as you undid your pants, hearing the zipper pull down. I felt your hips move as you rubbed yourself before placing the condom on.

"Ah, cold!" I heard you gasp and I laughed again, remembering that the lube should be warmed up first.

"You better not laugh at me. Your mouth's going to be too full to do that." You threatened in a low voice, husky with the lust of your erection. You roughly turned me to you and I whimpered and hesitated at what was to come next.

I watched as your eager member waited to be devoured by me, while you stealthily untied and arranged my hands behind your back, so that I was tied to you with your penis in my face, just inches from my mouth.

"Open wide, baby." You said and I grimaced, not liking that.

You laughed but ran your hands through my hair, coaxing me gently and I opened my lips, placing them around the tip of your penis. I softly mouthed it, pressing my lips tighter around the sensitive skin at the frenulum.

Moving your body into my mouth, you started to breathe harder and I slowly put your condom covered penis into my mouth more, pausing to see how far I could get it, as I started to push it toward the back of my mouth.

You moaned, unable to contain it any longer and your hips bucked slightly but I clung to you with my hands tied and shoved the rest of your length farther until it reached down into my throat. Your nails bit into my back, making the light welts from the flogger and crop, sting even more.

I had to pull away for a moment to catch my breath before I tried again with more force, so that my arms jerked you forward into my mouth, over and over. You were close to cumming and I could feel the lovely twitch of your penis in my mouth. I could just about hear your teeth biting into your soft lips as you moaned and I knew I was bringing you close to your climax, so I kept on, practically fucking your penis with my throat.

As your gasps and moans grew louder, so did mine and I moaned so that the vibrations traveled from my vocal cords into your hot, hard penis.

"Eat it, baby, eat it." You barely managed to say as you bit your lip and I gave your ass a tweak in response with my sharp fingernails.

"Oh yeah!" You gasped, misinterpreting my reprimand for pleasure.

I let the misunderstanding go and continued to bring you over the edge until I felt your legs almost give way. I pulled away and said, "Lie down over me," and you slowly bent your legs until we were both on our knees, then I slipped my legs between yours and pulled you over me, still with my hands tied behind you, until you crouched over my face.

I looked past you to make sure we were totally alone (which we were) before I pulled you down on me and took your penis all the way in my mouth again. This time you couldn't hold back any longer and you humped my mouth until at last you came, spurting your white fluid into the condom.

I pulled you to my side and we lay together for a moment, as I felt your chest heaving with your heavy, satisfied, breaths. You closed your eyes and stroked my neck and hair until finally my arms were getting sore in the tied position.

It took a moment to regain our balance but you got the knots undone quickly.

"That was amazing!" You laughed softly and I kissed your lovely lips again. I had only the waist rope on me now and you slowly took the condom off and tied it before putting it in the black plastic bag. You reached out for me and I snuggled into your arms as we rested for a bit on the sleeping bag. In the rafters the birds were cooing and flapping about.

"It's a great place for a scene fuck but it's not very romantic." I said.

"Yeah, I agree." You stretched and gave my back a quick rub. "That was fun."

"We didn't get to have sex or do anal yet…" I began and you shook your head and smiled.

"We better get back, it'll be dark soon and I don't want to be here at night."

"There's always next time." I offered mischievously.

"Yeah, definitely. When I'm in town again, we can do another trip like this." You nodded.

I got up and gathered my clothes, putting them on while you gathered the toys, condoms, gloves and lube into the black bag then rolled up the sleeping bag and tarp. I kept the rope on my waist, underneath my shirt, like a hidden secret no one else could know about.

It was a perfect time together and luckily we hadn't been interrupted by anyone. We walked back to the car, now seeing the evening shadows of the setting sun encroach upon us with the abandoned factory behind, like a monstrous guardian of the mountainous horizon.

We got into the car, kissing for a while before I put the key in.

"I know a place we can go to next time--it's near a creepy cemetery outside of town, off a ways from the highway. What do you think?" I asked.

"Sounds creepy and fun." You agreed and smiled.

I was already planning our next adventure together as I drove back, imagining all the wonderful, nasty fantasies we could play out in the future.

BETWEEN TWO ROOMS

By Ouroboros Sings

You're so impatient to begin, Matías, it almost makes me laugh.

"My, my, aren't you ready to be collared!"

"Yes, yes," you reply, "I'm ready to be possessed by you; I want you to take control and force me to do things that please you, because we're here to pleasure one anoth—"

"Shhhhhh, too much talking. You don't speak—I speak. Now listen to me, Matías, are you willing to submit to me, completely—to give up your will and your ego, to relinquish control of your flesh and your mind? To experience every sensation, to let yourself be carried away by that delicious, intoxicating pleasure-pain?"

"Yes, I give myself completely to you, Mistress!"

"Very well," I say, and buckle the leather collar around your neck. "I now possess you: from this moment on, you'll do everything I say, without question. Do you understand?"

"Yes, Mistress."

"Now, tell me the safe words."

"'Yellow' means 'ease up,' 'red' means 'full stop.'"

"Good boy," I smile, digging my fingers into your ass cheek as I kiss you on the lips; I then step back, and walk around you. You're excited by the sound of my black, spike-heel boots on the wood floor and the jingle of the heavy chrome chain that dangles between my nipple clamps. And you love those plain white briefs I'm wearing; your mind has already jumped forward to when you're falling asleep with my panties pressed to your nose… ohhh, those white panties… breathing in my scent left behind… you're drifting off…

Whack! You snap to attention at the sound of the riding crop against the doorframe "Now strip," I command, unsmiling, "and then stand over here." You hurriedly obey your Mistress; you place your clothes neatly on the table and then stand naked in the archway between the rooms; this is when you notice the chains…

I grab your right hand, quickly apply a heavy, black leather cuff, and hook you by the wrist to the chain in the upper-right corner of the doorframe. I grab your left hand, and deftly cuff and chain you to the upper-left corner. In a flash, I kneel down and chain you by the ankles to the lower corners. Your arms and legs are now spread wide—mmmm, this makes you nice and prone. I feel my clit pulsating.

Still kneeling, eye-level to your cock, I press my face against your crotch and breathe deep your scent, grazing your thigh with the cold chain hanging from my erect nipples. I part my lips and let your soft cock fall into my mouth; I roll you around with my tongue, swallow you down my throat, and then slowly… pull… you… out. You're still a little soft, and I have just the thing: I reach for a leather cock ring and snap it tight around the base of your shaft; your cock flinches, suddenly made aware of its predicament, but it still needs coaxing, so I grab a thicker metal ring: the ball stretcher. With one hand, I firmly grip your sack and pull down; with the other, I clamp on the heavy ring; its weight alone is enough to keep your sack stretched, but I add one more, teensy little torture—a small, but sufficiently heavy padlock through the loop.

You groan.

"Now you're properly dressed," I chirp, and set the weight swinging in motion. It pulls at your cock and balls as it swings back and forth, pulling back and forth… pulling, pulling…

***

I revel in hearing your groans; and I love how your gear looks, all strrrrretched out! I stand up, facing you; firmly gripping the riding crop in one hand, while I gently caress your cock with my other hand. I lean my face into your chest, flicker your nipple with my tongue, and then bite.

"Hoh!" you gasp.

"What was that, Matías? You say you want me to bite your harder?"

"Ahhh!!" you cry out. "Yeh– y– yellow!"

Teeth cede to tongue, and I soothingly lick your nipple; your whimpers turn to purrs. "There, there, my pet—I don't want to break you… yet." My tongue slips into your mouth to meet yours, dancing deep and wet. I step behind you; my hand gliding on the skin of your arm, your shoulder, down your back, patting your buttock; your eyes flutter and knees begin to buckle as you drift into…

Snap! You jump at the sting of the riding crop on your ass.

Snap-snap-snap, followed by a gentle caress. Then your thighs, snap-snap! "Ahhh!!" you moan. "Too much?" "No!! It's wonderful!" you cry out!

Exchanging the riding crop for a paddle, I reach around to your front and rub your cock with the fake fur side. So soft, like a little black kitten on your hard phallus. I bring the paddle back around to your backside, and rub your ass cheeks with the fur. You're purring again…

Whack! The hard leather side stings mightily. Three. More. Hard. Hits.

You cry out, "own me, please, Mistress! Possess my ass; oh, please!" "Is that what you want, Matías?" "Yes!" "Are you certain you're ready to submit yourself to me, to open yourself wide, make yourself absolutely vulnerable to my hand?" "God yes, please, please, possess my ass! Please, Mistress, let me give myself to you!"

"Very well."

Your rock-hard cock jumps at the stretch and snap of neoprene gloves. Your ass cheeks tighten at the squirting sound of lube. Your sphincter puckers at the touch of my wet, gloved finger. I rub and gently press my finger against your warm asshole; I want to dive right in, but I know I must be gentle.

"Breathe, Matías." My finger rubs back and forth from your stretched balls, across your anus, up your crack. "Take a deep breath in…" You fill your lungs with the scent of incense mixed with sweat. "Now breathe out…" And as you exhale, my lubed finger slips into your asshole.

"Ohhhhhhhh," you moan, as I work my finger in and out, slowly twisting, twirling, and probing. I love the feel of your silky, hot rectum gripping and relaxing, gripping and relaxing.

And now, two fingers. "Hohhhhhhhh," you groan. Two fingers pushing, stretching, probing deeper. "Are you enjoying this, Matías?" "Yeh– y– yes, oh yes! You've possessed my asshole!"

"No, my dear pet, I haven't possessed you yet—" as I pull out. "But, I am about to…"

***

The sound of more squirting lube…

I lean into you, whisper into your year, "Now, Matías. Now I am going to possess your asshole." And with that, I take one hand and spread your cheeks wide open; with the other, I pinch all my fingers together, narrowing my hand as much as possible. I touch the tips to your asshole, and then slowly, gently, ever so carefully press. Little by little, the tight ring of your sphincter relaxes; slowly, slowly, it loosens its grip; slowly, slowly, it relinquishes its power. "Ahhh, there you go; good boy, Matías." Your sphincter finally gives in to me; your ass finally succumbs, and submits to the invasion of my hand.

I am reaching inside you, Matías. You have trusted me enough to allow me into that most deeply protected, vulnerable place inside you. My hand, Matías—my hand is in your ass, gently rolling inside you, in and out, softly twisting, massaging your prostate; I am reaching inside you, occupying your cave; I am completely and utterly possessing your ass, possessing your body, possessing your entire psyche.

As I continue with one hand, pushing in, drawing out, gently twisting and rolling, with my free hand I caress your back, rubbing up and down your spine. You are like a glove, Matías—a glove that is alive and breathing and gasping. My free hand reaches between your legs and fondles your balls. Gently massaging and squeezing your sack that is already so very sensitive from the pressure of the ball stretcher. I then reach up and caress your granite-hard cock. Oh my god, Matías, you are so fucking hard. Your glans is deepening red with excitement; a beautiful pearl of cum is forming on the tip. I gently, expertly fist your ass, and start to give you a handjob, rubbing up and down your heavy shaft, when suddenly—

"Ruh– re- red!!!" you shout.

I freeze in place.

"Matías, are you OK? Am I hurting you?"

"N-– no. No, but…"

"What is it, Matías?"

"It's fantastic! God, your fantastic, but I don't want to come—I was about to come, and I don't want to. Not yet. Not before I fuck you in your ass."

The thought warms my heart like you cannot imagine! I very gently pull out of your ass, remove the gloves, and clean my hands with cucumber-scented wipes. With more wipes, I clean your ass, so gently, lovingly. I kneel down and release your ankle cuffs, and then unclamp the ball stretcher; your cock flinches at its sudden, stinging freedom. As I stand up, I kiss your calves, I kiss the backs of your knees, I kiss the backs of your thighs, I kiss your ass cheeks, kiss your anus, I kiss the base of your spine, I kiss the small of your back, I kiss you between your shoulder blades, I kiss the nape of your neck.

I reach up and release you from the wrist cuffs, gently supporting your weakened arms. And now, you stand there eyeing me as you rub the circulation back into your muscles, while I stand before you, no longer the dominatrix, but the submissive.

No longer the predator, but the prey.

"Take off your panties," you order me in a surprisingly calm, firm voice.

I remove my white panties; the crotch is absolutely soaked through with my nectar. With both hands, I raise them up for you to sniff. Having received your smiling groan of approval, I then place the white panties over your head and arrange them so that the crotch lies across your face. You feel my wetness stick to your lips; you breathe in my heady, musky scent.

I finish dressing you with a condom and for a moment, lose myself in caressing your steel cock and clenched scrotum.

You grab the chain hanging from my nipple clamps, pull up hard and drag me across the room. It hurts—oh, how it hurts—I moan in delicious pain. Seeing how angry red my nipples are, you remove the clamps, which make me cry out in even more pain, so tender they now are. Thus, as did I with you, you calm the fire with loving, gentle strokes of your tongue.

"Now turn around, face the bed, and get on your hands and knees." I obey my Master. With my ass up and facing you, I suddenly feel so open, so vulnerable. A trickle of juice escapes my flower; its petals swollen with excitement. You knock my knees further apart; I feel off balance—it underscores the fact that I am no longer in control.

Rather than reach for the lube, you suddenly plunge a hand into my flower, shoving it in and out quite violently. You start ramming my pussy hard and fast; I am moaning loudly, almost animal-like, with pleasure. "Oh, god! Ohhhhhh, godddddd!" Sensing that I'm nearly coming, you pull out, wait a moment for me to gain my composure, and then you rub your dripping hand all over my asshole. I gasp as your finger enters me.

Oh no, you pulled out—no no no, why did you stop? I want you in me so bad!

And so…

I get my wish—your engorged cock drives into my ass as my moans turn to screams turn to tears…

"Am I hurting you, Mistress?" "No! Christ, don't you dare stop!!!"

With every thrust of your cock in my ass, I cry out. With every thrust of your cock in my ass, I feel your balls slap against me. With every thrust of your cock in my ass, I meet you with the thrust of my pelvis.

"Harder—fuck me harder! Slam into me, baby! Oh God!!!"

You slam and slam and slam into me. Your voice grows savage and guttural, "uh-uh-rrrraaaaaaaa!" as your body stiffens and shakes and you come like a fire hose into my ass. You collapse onto my quaking, writhing body; I've come so hard that I flinch uncontrollably. I feel your entire weight pressing down on me; I feel your cock still pumping into me. My body won't be still; my body still undulates, and I gasp for air…

Slowly, slowly we stop shaking, you and I. Our panting starts to normalize into calm, rhythmic breaths; our pounding heartbeats slow.

You kiss the back of my neck and then roll yourself and me, as one, onto our sides—your arms are wrapped tightly around me; your cock is still inside me as we drift… as we… we drift… off… to sleep.

TATAMI AND WOOD

By Ev Joy Lokadottr

She knelt in seiza on the tatami mat, trembling. Biting her lower lip, eyes downcast, she studied the pattern of the woven rushes. One straw had a dark ring around it near the edge of the mat she was currently sitting on, and her eyes kept getting drawn back to it.

She drew in one breath, through her nose, out her mouth, and then another. The last student, aside from her, had left about 5 minutes ago. It felt like 5 hours.

Silence had fallen over the dojo like a woolen blanket, the only sound her breathing, which was a little too fast, and the slow, measured "pat, pat, pat" of her sensei's feet as he walked to the door. Then there was the lock, it's metal bolt scraping as it slid home, and the whisper of curtains closing.

Then his feet on the floor, getting closer, behind her. Her sensei, breathing in. And her world was filled with his rich, deep voice, surrounding her, enfolding her, full and intimate, touching her deep inside

"Kohai..."

His fingertips brushed a stray hair from her face, tucking it behind her ear. A quivering whimper escaped her lips.

"Kohai."

"Osu?" she breathed.

"Why are you afraid? You have nothing to lose. I have taken you, and you are mine. All of you. Even your life is mine. Always. Yes, there will be pain, but that is mine as well."

She squeezed her eyes shut, balling her hands into fists.

"Or do you doubt? Do you need another lesson?"

"No, sensei," her shoulders hunched, hands loose again, palms up, imploring, "please."

“I decide. Always.”

"Osu."

"Now stand, and take off your pants and panties. Fold them properly, and put them on the bench there. Then, go to the middle of the mats, and wait for me there."

"Osu," and she rose, a little unsteady on her feet, heart hammering. She disrobed and placed her clothing where he had instructed her to, then stood in the middle of the mat, feet together, hands pressed to her sides.

He walked into his office, bowing as he left the mats, and picked something up. He returned, bowing again, holding the object behind his back.

"Yoi"

He stalked around her, pausing to drink in the scent of the nape of her neck, so close that all the little hairs stood up.

A hand snaked around her waist, grasping her wrist and pulling it behind her back. Coils of rope slid around her arm, and then he grabbed the other wrist and did the same, binding her limbs behind her back.

Sensei tangled his fist in his kohai's hair and pulled her head towards him until she was arching her back, held upright by his other strong hand, grasping her bound wrists.

"Your kicks are weak. We're going to work on them a little tonight. Osu?"

"Osu, sensei."

He moved in front of her again, and said, "Rei."

They bowed, her trying her best to not topple forward.

"Hajime," and he raised his hands into a guard position.

"Wait, you get to punch me?"

"My kicks are fine."

He threw a slow cross, and she twisted her body, moving away from the blow, hopping a little.

"Come on, kohai," he growled, thumping her chest with a nasty jab, "Show me your kicks. Mawashi Geri! Both sides!"

She threw a roundhouse kick, then another, trying to catch him in the thigh or the side with her shin. He effortlessly blocked her, and on her fifth kick, he grabbed her ankle, lifting her leg high, almost toppling her over.

He stepped forward, still holding her leg high, and rammed two fingers deep inside her exposed pussy. She screamed, but he would not let her go. She could not struggle, for fear of falling.

"Now that's a sweet little cunt," he purred, "I like how you showed it to me. So slow... you must have wanted this."

He stepped back, suddenly, and dropped her leg.

"Maybe I'm giving you too much structure? Maybe you're not inspired enough. Maybe I'm boring you... Perhaps you need more motivation?"

He advanced on her with a flurry of blows. She stumbled backwards, trying to block with her knees as best she could. Sensei snapped his hand out, grabbing hold of the front of her gi and yanking it open.

"You're always showing off your tits in class. I know you want me to see them. Show me." He shoved his hand into her bra and pulled out her breast, squeezing it.

Then he began to strike her again. And again. And again. Desperate now, she tried to kick him, hard. He caught her leg again and pushed her down on her side.

Slowly, gracefully, he lowered himself until his body was inches away from her own, the tips of his belt trailing over her thigh. She could feel the radiating heat of his body, and his breath on her face in that moment of stillness as he suspended himself over her.

Then, quick like a strike, he was on her, pressing her down, snarling, his sharp teeth gripping the tender flesh of her throat. She moaned, and he opened his jaws, trailing the tip of his tongue up her neck, along the line of her jaw, over her lips. His hand slid up along her back, and he grabbed a fistful of her hair, forcing her head to tilt towards him.

He grinned, and he said "I want to devour you."

And then he kissed her. Not the soft, tentative kiss of a shy lover. It was rough, forceful, parting her lips and driving his tongue into her, catching her mouth with the very tip of a tooth, kissing her as if he would swallow her.

He was so fierce. So frightening. Powerful. Something inside of her thrilled at it. She felt so confused. This was bad, right? This was wrong? But she had come back. She had stayed, because he'd told her to. He loosened his grip on her hair, and then began to stroke head. His lips withdrew from her own, and she felt almost empty. His hand moved to her cheek, lightly trailing his nails up the side of her cheek, over her brow. She looked into his eyes. Intense, pale grey and stormy, like none she'd ever seen before. She felt as if she could lose herself in them. As if she could drift away...

"There... there. That's a good girl. Let go. You are mine now. Let go. Open yourself to me. I will take care of you. And I will also take you. Whenever, however I want. Do you understand, kohai?"

"Osu... Osu sensei."

I've brought a little surprise for you, my kohai. Lie still, now."

The woven straw of the tatami mat pressed into her cheek.

His body left hers, and she felt herself adrift, chilled, almost... yearning. Yearning for that strength, that power, that deep and mesmerizing voice, urging her to open herself to him, to drop all of her defenses, to yield.

He returned, sitting on the mat in front of her. To her, he presented an object: gleaming, polished wood, smooth and sculpted in the shape of two phalluses intertwined like serpentine creatures.

"You will take everything I want you to. You will fulfill my every desire. You shall do this, because it is MY will that you serve me in this way. Do you understand, kohai? The choice is not yours. Release yourself from the bonds of your fears, from the chains of your inhibitions. Under my hand, you will soar."

"OSU," the carved wood frightened her, and yet, the floaty feeling intensified, as if the world was gently falling away, as it nothing existed but her sensei, her self, which was tethered to him, and that thing in his hand.

His fingertips ran down her body, leaving a trail of shivering goosebumps, the sensation intensified when they touched upon her bare thighs. He reached the tender back of her knee, and bent her leg up toward her chest. Then, while she laid on her side, he knelt between her legs, so close to the soft pink lips of her exposed womanhood.

His empty hand flew, barely striking her flesh, his fingers curling, clamping down on her nether lips. "This is *mine*," he growled, the promise of violence stirring just below the surface. His eyes gleamed, steel and lightning, and she saw in him the hungry beast, held so carefully at bay so much of the time, flashing fang and claw behind his gaze.

Then, as lightly as the last moment had been rough, he spread open her trembling lips, pressing his forearm down on her thigh, keeping her legs in place.

"You may deny it, but it's futile. Your body betrays you, exposing your true desires. You are slick, and wet, kohai. You want it. You want the pleasure. You want the pain, You want to take it all for me. This is true, this is real. This is all that is real. Breathe. Breathe with me. Understand that you cannot stop this. Any of this. Surrender to it. It is coming, and you may scream, but you will love it. You will crave it."

The wooden carving pressed against her warm, wet opening, hard and unyielding against her soft flesh. It's shape was alien, twin heads sinking into her, stretching her, relentlessly pressing deeper and deeper. She squirmed and tightened all her muscles, resisting, but…

"Easy… easy… shhhhh... let it go, open yourself, relax. It will only hurt you more if you do not. Surrender. Give yourself to me. Let it happen. Relax. Breathe."

She let out a breath she didn't know she was holding. She knew he was telling the truth. He wasn't stopping. She felt soft, languid, almost, but the sensation of the thing inside of her was so intense. The spiraled double cock went deeper inside of her, and he began to twist it, and then plunge it in and out. It was so hard, so thick, she almost couldn't bear it. Almost. She moaned, and then she began to scream, and writhe, and her cunt began to tighten. It hurt, but also... also it felt so good.

A wave began to rise deep within her. Her cries took on a frantic, urgent pitch, and he hissed "Yessssss... cum for me. Cum!"

The orgasm tore through her, and a ragged scream burst out of her as she arched her back, bucking and squeezing.

"Again! Cum!"

And again she came. He yanked it out of her, and an aftershock of pleasure and pain rolled through her. The carving glistened with her juices. He held it up to his face and breathed in the scent on it, eyes half-lidded, savoring the smell of her.

"You see? Mine."

He carried it away, and then returned to her, unbinding her wrists. Tenderly, he rubbed them.

"I don't want to break my favorite toy. Now, get on your hands and knees. It's time to work those muscles, and teach you about weapons..."

Sensei stood a bo staff in his hand. Only... it was not a normal bo staff, for on one end there was carved a wooden sphere, wider by far than the slender staff itself.

"Strength. Timing. Control. Skill. Power. Focus. Flow. You must learn all of these things, kohai. And I will train you."

"Osu, sensei."

Her cunt was still pulsing with the heat of her orgasm, still sore from the rough penetration.

"You fear the bo. When I picked it up, you retreated. It's rare for you to retreat, my kohai. You have spirit and heart, but you fear this more than most men. I wonder why?"

"I... I don't know sensei. It intimidates me."

"It is not the weapon that should concern you. It is the hand that wields it. As my hand does now."

He ran the narrow tip of the bo down her spine, and then lifted it away. She heard the swooping sound of it spinning, and cringed.

"But you will learn. You will know it. And then you will only fear it when I want you to."

He came down on one knee behind her, and then she felt it- the ball at the end of the bo, pressing against her, pressing into her, penetrating her. It was big, and it stretched her cunt out even more than it had been before. She dug her fingers into the mat, but still he pushed, until with a kind of a pop, it was inside of her.

"Now... hold it."

She couldn't help but do so, for she knew it would stretch and hurt just as much coming out as it did going in. He flowed to his feet, and she felt the weight of it inside her, the shaft beyond the ball rising like a lever. He reached behind him, and picked up something that was leaning against the wall. With a loud CRACK, she felt the sting of bamboo striking her buttocks! She yelped and jerked, but the ball pulled against her opening, forcing her to still herself. He had a shinai.

"Crawl. Crawl for me. Remember, if you try to move away, it will be painful. If you start to lag, I will beat you. Although... I may beat you anyway."

And so she crawled, slowly, carefully.

"Yes, move that ass... I love the way you look, crawling. I love the rock of your hips. I love the feel of your cunt gripping my staff. I'll use that tight fuck hole for my pleasure before I let you go. But you will still be mine when I do. I will never let you go completely. Osu?"

"Osu."

"Now, faster! Move!"

And he struck her with the shinai, again and again, goading her forward as she crawled, the ball and the staff hard and unforgiving inside of her.

"Focus! Focus, kohai, focus..." and he made her crawl all the way around the mats, once, twice, and a third time.

"Now, stop."

He eased the ball out of her. She winced and whined wordlessly, but out it came.

"Seiza."

She rose up on her knees, and then sat on her heels, hands on her thighs.

"Bow."

She placed her left hand on the floor in front of her knees, and then her right, first fingers touching together. Then she lowered her head and her elbows to the ground. The mat creaked lightly as he sank down behind her. She heard the rustle of the thick cotton cloth of his gi, and then she felt it- the hot, hard, velvety-steelhead of his cock, pressing against her aching, swollen pussy.

"Strength. Control. I know I stretched you out, my kohai. My little fuck bitch. But I know that you will be tight for me..."

And he rammed his cock into her, deep, deep inside, down to the hilt of him, striking her cervix. Mercilessly, he slamfucked her, over and over and over again, thrusting with those powerful hips, using the force of his entire body to drive himself into her. Beating her from the inside.

"Take it. Take it for me! Take it and cum!"

Her body obeyed. Her spirit obeyed. She came, over and over and over again. His thrusts came harder, faster, almost out of control, and he groaned, and then roared, roared so the walls seemed to shake, and her heart rattled in its cage of bone, and her cunt clamped down as he filled her with his hot seed.

He pulled out and rocked back on his heels, then growled, "Now cum! Cum hard! Let it go, let it out, cum for me!"

She came, and with a shocked cry, her pleasure poured out, staining the mats wet with their cum pouring over the straw, singing into the floor. She was his.

BTLAZOLTEOTL IN THE LANGUAGE OF HINDUISM AND ASATRU

Or: Because I Do Not Know Your Language Well Enough Yet
By Pope Uncommon the Dainty

Concerning the performance of sacred purification ritual using
your own urine in the place of water:
Know
that human is far too small a word
for what you are,
O weird,
please,
die teased and wanting in the fullness of the degradation of life,
liquid skin and counted breath,
a final fetishistic meditation in every blink--
O weird--
they'll tell you that Brahma
blinks
and that this dreaming world disappears
when self-seeing light fills open eyes,
juicy and sweet--
O weird--
write your own disturbing dictionary.
Note that "human"

from the Latin "humandus,"
that which must be buried,
gives you your immortality
and that weird once meant
fate and eventual failure
to the Vikings, their gods dying
in the fullness of the degradation of life,
liquid skin and counted breath wilting victorious
before enemy giants.
Only Odin's ravens
remained to feast
on divine eyeballs
juicy and sweet
(their names were Thought and Memory)--
None of these words are large enough to fit you,
O weird,
lower your swollen and sickened mouth to your abdomen
use your teeth
to burrow past intestines
find that still place
where no wind blows
where your breath goes
to die, where your power lies,
that dirty golden lake
filled with the ghosts of your one-celled ancestors.
Drink deep.
Brahma
blinks.
I bless you, O weird:
may your defining tongue taste
like fertile diarrhea.
You are most yourself when you are ground,
unsure of your shape and freeing,
fleeing.
These rites should fill you with terror--
you are holy
you are free
you are kink and magickal talisman.
Enter this temple now,
filled with this lowest
priestly power.

We are ravenous gods

when we are subhuman,
feasting on divine eyeballs
juicy and sweet.

Liquid skin
and counted breath.

We are rising up in reverse.

BEAU'S TURN

By Kathleen Mahnke

I've always been a Dom. Before I had any idea BDSM existed, I showed affection by gently pulling my love's hair and arousal by roughly pulling it back and kissing her until she couldn't breathe. By the time most women discover lingerie and cocktails; I was tying down lovers and forcing them to scream out their passion and need.

It wasn't any drive to prove superiority, so much as an instinctual expression of it. Just like an awkward teenager might impulsively lean into a sloppy kiss, I tied my first love's hands above her head and went down on her in the stall of our high school's bathroom. The purple bite marks against her umber skin turned me on for a week, and their fading left a strange sense of mourning in my heart.

Life moves forward, and loves slip away. So many people I've met in the BDSM scene talk about sex with the casual attachment you might feel toward drinking coffee or getting your car's oil changed. Love, lust, and power have always been interconnected to me. Yes, some loves only last a night, but I cannot hold a person's passion, adoration, and obedience in my hand without also surrendering a part of myself.

Nothing matches the intoxication of complete intimacy, with every barrier torn, ripped, and beaten down. Tonight, I feared it.

While I have had many loves and lovers, nothing came close to my connection with Beauregard Mathis. Was it the magic-fueled moment I looked into his soul? Was it because my powers of empathically picking up on his emotions, especially passionate emotions, had become so much stronger as I grew in my magic?

More than a little of my feelings came from having stood next to him in battle. Knowing that he would lay down his life for me stripped away any pretext of distance or safety in my heart. It was not just like being naked. It was like stripping away my skin and having every nerve exposed to the feelings that moved in the air between us.

Beauregard was the only lover I had never dominated, until tonight. Truth flooded me as ice spread in my stomach. My hand trembled as I forced myself to sit, poised and waiting.

I am used to people seeking me out, and sacrificing to be with me. Even my now-billionaire ex-husband had been on the bottom and glad to be tied down. With Beau… I had been the aggressor. To be more honest, I had been drawn to him beyond boundaries.

Pride and positions had no place in the passion I felt next to him. Gravity has less pull on me than this man. I became a switch the first time we made love. In our time together it was always me who reached out, who needed, craved, and was willing to give in order to receive. In fact, mentioning the strange newness of it all had led to tonight.

I lay on Beauregard's chest, coated in sweat and feeling dizzy satiation from my toes to my soul. "It's strange really."

"Hm?" Beau shifted his weight back and pulled me until I was laying on him instead of next to him.

"Everyone else I've ever been with I've been on top." I sleepily cozzied against him.

"You are on top quite a bit." He played his fingers through my hair and scratched my head. I never should have told him my weakness.

I half-purred. "Not like that, silly man."

"Is there a different way to be on top? Would you enjoy riding more often, perhaps?" His face showed his genuine confusion.

I laughed. It was easy; with how much Beauregard pleased me and how well he knew my body to forget that despite his older age, I had more experience with sexuality outside traditional ranges. "Being on top in a kinky way."

He took time to process and puzzle. I could feel his uncertainty. "Kinky way, my dear?"

It was my turn to reach up, play his silver and white hair through my fingers, and scratch his scalp. "Well, you know I tend more to the naughty side than you do…"

"Out with it, Maria. Every time to try to soften statements it terrifies me." He hugged me to him, but I felt worry creep into his spirit. I could not blame Beau. The few times I had been afraid to speak plainly with him, it involved intensely dangerous situations.

Maybe I was a little afraid as well. "I love rough loving."

"I have noticed." He breathed out and his usual deep calm enveloped me. "Do I need to be rougher? You know I would provide any need…" He left off and looked at me, seeming to connect pieces.

I confirmed. "You are the first lover I haven't been rough to… No. I mean." It was suddenly me who felt nervous. We fit so well together as things were. I couldn't imagine this solid old warrior in any of the positions I had put past flings. He was not someone I could simply overpower, or drink in with rash abandon. Part of why I found myself in love with Beauregard was his nearly infinite strength, his core of SELF that could not be budged, broken, or overcome.

"You are plenty rough with me. My back remembers you every time you go home." He kissed the top of my head. "What is troubling you, Maria?"

"We fit. I fall against you. You pull me closer and crush me into your power. I let you rip into me, because I need it." I arched up so Beau and I could talk face to face. "You come from a world… a time so different from mine. Your love was always within those bounds. You had a wife. A single love…" I saw the sadness at her mention and paused, trying to find where to start over from. "You are used to being "the man" in a different way. You lead, shoulders squared. You shelter me, even when I hate it. You expect to make every call, and have your words weigh something. And they do. And you are the best of all those qualities that so many men have abused.

I love everything about you. And I don't want to ask you to change any of it. I don't want you to be like my pretty club boys who are used to being flexible in their own beautiful way. I want you to be you. I just…" It all came spilling out of my mouth without thought or planning. I had never thought of Beauregard as a possible submissive, yet, now the thought was in my mind, it was sinking into my heart. What mistress would not want the surrender of the most beautiful lover she had known?

Beauregard was silent. His eyes met mine, and he took in what I said. After a few moments he replied. "You came into my home and asked me to turn my world upside down mentoring you. I did. You… shared yourself in a way I was not at first comfortable with, but I do not regret it, and in fact am grateful every day that you chose to. You demanded I walk into a deadly situation because it was the right thing to do. Not only did I comply, I almost ended up dead trying to make sure you and your loved ones got out. Now you are worried there is something sexual you cannot ask of me?"

It was my time to think. Beauregard gave me quiet space. I love how considerate he is. "It does sound silly out loud."

"It means that much to you." Beauregard's words rang true.

I had held back a part of myself because it was too sensitive, too exposed. I already love this man too much, too wildly, and too deeply. Maybe I had opened up a new side of myself, but I had also hidden away who I am. "Yes."

"Then it is something you should, or rather, we should do." And like so many things Beauregard said, that was that. We both relaxed, cuddled, wiggled in our separate directions, reached out to touch each other, and went to sleep.

Now I sat at my vanity and waited. I laughed. It was the first time Beauregard was coming to my house that I wasn't shot in the head or near-death from a supernatural viper bite. The laughter broke through my nervousness and I got up to stretch.

Candles were lit, and positioned on silver trays, for both safety and the reflected glow against old metal. My layers of blankets were folded and hidden under the bed. Only sheets remained.

I am normally a black bra and matching panties kind of woman. Beauregard had once mentioned "You'd look pretty in a nice, feminine blue." Tonight I wore an Edwardian style corset in a dark blue shantung silk. I admired how tight it pulled at my waist, and how full my cleavage looked. My stockings were white and Cuban-style; nearly transparent except where the solid white line highlighted the back of my leg. The contrast between pale stockings and my tan thighs pleased me. My heels were high, but ankle straps and perfect craftsmanship created a perfect balance. My long hair was coiled and swept up so it would not get tangled and in the way when I beat the man I loved.

My self-satisfaction paused as I heard my front door open. Steps sounded up the stairs. Then there was scuffling followed by silence. I watched the clock and waited three full minutes before opening the door.

Beauregard was there on his knees.

Beauregard had tendrils of trepidation in the air around him. I brushed my fingers through his wavy silver hair. Tenderness threatened my resolve for half a breath. I dug my fingers down to his scalp and pulled hard. He could follow or resist, but I used enough force that resisting would have led to a fistful of Beauregard's hair being pulled out by the root.

He followed me in on his knees. I strutted in, hips swinging, my lover crawling behind. I pulled his head to the mattress, leading him to lay against it with his knees on the floor. My fingers traced over his muscular shoulders and I leaned close enough that my breasts brushed his upper back. "I thought of going soft on you." I scratched down his scalp, traced the lines beside his spine with my nails, and buried my talons in the flesh of his ass. "I knew it would be wrong to soften your sacrifice." Leaned my head against his. "I am grateful for what you are choosing to share. I respect your gift."

Beauregard nodded. I could feel his resolve. I got down on the floor beside him and gave him a hug. I moved my arm up to gently choke him in the crook of my elbow; playfully leading his head to my chest as I alternately teased and restricted his air flow. My other hand petted softly down his back, and then firmly smacked his ass.

He jumped slightly, but settled back into my threatening embrace. I wondered if It was the first time he had been spanked. Then, I spanked him again. His body jolted again, but not enough to shift his position.

I kissed his ear, then spanked him, nibbled his shoulder, then spanked him, tightened my grip on his throat, then spanked him. His body involuntarily rocked away from each strike. After each impact he settled deeper into the rhythm of accepting my loving violence.

My force deepened with each strike. Soon Beau showed no surprise at the impact, but his body rocked forward from the force. My fingers began to tingle and his ass turned red. My pussy got wet.

The gentle kisses that had countered each strike became vicious bites. I heard myself growl against his skin as my teeth went deeper. Beau's own soft moan reached deep inside me and made me smile.

I reached down his back again. The touch was not only gentle, but so soft it could barely be felt. Down his shoulders, his shoulder blades, over the ropey muscles to each side of his spine, to the soft dip that marks even the strongest back. I traced the lines of his butt, smiling as he arched slightly to my touch, then traced between his cheeks, reaching between his legs and teasing his balls with feather-soft touch.

Beauregard leaned forward slightly, looking back at me less to question, and more to see what was happening. I reached further, and felt him hard from the abuse and teasing. Beau drew in a breath as if to say something, perhaps to explain his arousal after being spanked on his knees. I met his eyes with mine and shook my head. He nodded slightly and laid his face against the sheet again.

I teased his shaft with the same soft touch I had played over his back. His breathing had become more strained. With slow, almost imperceptible intention I traced circles around his shaft and up to the head of his cock.

Beauregard moaned. It was his first indiscretion. I had given strict instructions, mostly because I looked forward to disciplining him when he could not obey.

I smacked his ass sharply and he braced against it. I had to stay behind Beauregard so he would not see my widening smile. He moved obediently as I grabbed his shoulders and led him to get up, then stretch face down crosswise on my bed.

"You know I am going to punish you." I ran a teasing finger slowly over his calf.

"Yes Mar-" Beauregard could not get out the word before I slapped the back of his leg harshly.

"No speaking, remember?" Beau nodded silently and I rewarded him with soft pets up his inner thigh. "Now, my love. Let us see if you can remain silent."

The moment of truth had come. I was not nervous like someone who might fail, but nervous like someone who stood on a cliff, prepared to jump into the void in a glider. I was ready to fly. Somehow, I knew Beauregard was also.

I tied a sash of silk over Beau's eyes, making sure there were no gaps, and cinching it tight before knotting it behind his head. I then led him to lay face down again. Ropes lay under the bed, prepared and ready as I tied first Beau's hands (making sure multiple loops distributed the tension,) then his ankles.

The bed itself created a frame, much like I might stretch a canvas.

After tying his arms and legs crosswise, I picked up the lengths of rope left to the head and foot of the bed and bound them against the first set, so that it looked like Beauregard was caught in a net, helpless against a network of thick cording.

I knew it was an illusion. Beau could summon his power to break the bed, could make the ropes age and fray around him, or could simply ask to be let go. I knew he would not. Beau's real bindings were ones of willingness.

The thought left me breathless. I decided to slip the blindfold off, just for a few moments. I unceremoniously threw a pillow on the floor near Beauregard's head and sat on it, legs spread. Beau remained obedient and silent. His eyes traveled over me, and I arched back, letting him see how wet I was. I took the double-headed dildo I had purchased just for this night and began playing it in and out of my pussy.

At first his eye widened at the sight. At least part of it was nervousness over what he had agreed to try. More of his expression was desire. I started out teasing him, but soon allowed myself time to relax into the pleasure of my own fucking.

It felt oddly stimulating to let Beau watch me like this. Though we have had sex many times, it was voyeuristic and evil, selfish, and a bit impersonal. It felt like having a stranger watch me fuck from afar. At the same time, the delicious knowledge it was my love made it feel dangerous.

I more fully understood how frightened I had been to step outside his view of me. While I had not hesitated to show him my soul, I had withheld the depravity of my sexual desires as though always falling into him would shield me from judgment. Now, I was fully spread and fucked myself in my own way. I let him watch.

The pleasure and fear made a delicious cocktail. Soon, I was halfway to orgasm. Beau's eyes met mine and I smiled, and then let him feel it.

While I am the empath, he has always been open to the emotions I share with him. A wicked laugh left my lips as I let him feel what I did. Love played a subtle undertone that was almost flooded by physical pleasure. His breathing grew heavier as He felt not only my excitement, but the sensation of having a wet cunt stuffed full, knowing your love watches, feeling the last few barriers ripping away and knowing there is no going back.

I let him enjoy with me as I leaned back and traced my fingers over my throat. He shared as I reached my hand down and started pushing the toy between my legs again, more violently this time. We shared a rough edge, and the knowledge that what we were doing could not be undone.

The temptation to hold back came to me. His soft moan let me know Beau needed this. I stretched out the moment. Beauregard's lust and excitement washed through me as I reached my own climax. The lines between my own excitement and his blurred.

For a few breaths of time there was nothing but jagged pleasure, flavored with shame, wild abandon, and discovery. My body convulsed and the rough void took me.

It was an eternity before I remembered to breathe. Beau was staring at me with intense silence. I reached for my harness and intentionally buckled it up, letting him watch like it was a promise.

My instincts urged me to flip him over and ride him. I wanted to simply let my passion take me to the next step. Tonight was not an average night, and such self-indulgence would not do justice to the ritual.

After a few deep breaths, and some stern self-control, I leaned forward. Instead of kissing Beauregard and drinking in his comfort and strength, I bit him on the shoulder. At first I was gentle. It was a disoriented gesture born of the fuzzy after-pleasure of my orgasm.

Soon, my teeth sunk deeper. I stopped short of drawing blood, but not by much. Beau reflexively grounded himself. I could feel the pain of my bite flowing away into the deep roots that nourish Beauregard's power.

I considered telling him to stop. He would. But this night was about exposing all of ourselves. He didn't need to let go of his power. I needed to hurt him enough to exceed it.

He seemed to sense my intention. I realized I had left the channel of emotion open between us. Maybe that was also part of what we needed to share. I gently kissed his cheek. Beau nodded, as if we were about to start a duel and he was ready.

I slapped him across the jaw. Then I stood up and reached for my crop. It was a wicked rubber core model I had gotten at a shop that sold horse gear. Rather than using the small popper at the end, I wielded it more like a cane.

It swished through the air and bounded back on itself. Once I had the feel I turned to Beau and started in on his shoulders. The thick muscles could take deep strikes. I started with a few vicious strokes, and then settled into a rhythm. Rough, rough, rough, soft… I slowly, sadistically painted his body with red lines.

Down his back, over his ass. Rough, rough, rough, soft… I avoided the tender areas. For all his magic, I did not know if kidney strikes would have some damaging effect like they do in humans. For the areas of muscle, there was no mercy.

Beyond his back, over his ass, and down his legs, I painted Beauregard in delicious red welts. When his entire body was alive with pain and sensation I came up the other side. It began to look like a herringbone pattern of red V's decorating his skin.

Beyond the welts, I could feel Beauregard's pain. It telegraphed to me through our link. He dropped the stoic outer layers and began at first to sharply intake his breath, then to moan, and then groan under the repetitive strikes.

I struck harder. The sharp sting of the rubber seemed to drain away beneath his strength, but the impact carried through. I smiled. Our link went both ways. While I felt Beauregard's pain, I understood it. I increased it. Each blow followed through and rocked the foundations of his strength.

The strikes fell like rain. They went deep like a massage. They hurt like hell.

I found myself poised over the most beautiful human I had ever known. He was even more beautiful now. Red stripes made lace over his skin. I knelt next to him. The heat of angry muscles could be felt from inches away. His resolve was deep, but he ached.

The sensations of my kisses were multiplied by the tenderness of his tortured body. Beau had resisted calling out in pain. He had remained mostly still and stoic through the beating. Now he moaned openly and arched to my mouth.

Somehow I was crying. My salt tears burned. My kisses flowed over every inch of my exposed lover's flesh. My breasts felt searing heat as I lay against his back and stretched out over Beauregard's body.

He tensed and I realized my strap-on had landed between his legs. I smiled and nuzzled his shoulder.

"It is alright Maria, I promised." Beauregard's voice felt surprising after a small, intimate eternity of silence broken only by the sounds of heavy breaths and struck flesh.

I soaked up the comfort and smiled at his words. "Not quite yet, but you are fucking beautiful."

Why had I held back? How foolish was it to be scared? I devoured Beau's body with loving abandon. I hugged, caressed, and kissed every inch of his back. I licked up the angry welts on the back of his legs (but not behind the knees, of course.)

Somehow I gravitated back to that cute butt of his. A few weeks ago I never would have described it that way. Beauregard was manly. He was strong. I may have thought he had a great ass, but a cute butt? Beau was much too dignified for such a description.

Now I kissed it, licked it, and playfully bit over the red stripes I had left. Beau writhed. A simple shift of the hips, but I loved it.

I grabbed both sides and licked down the middle. His gasp delighted me. How had I never? I straddled his back and leaned forward.

My tongue traced down between his cheeks. I tasted sweat and faint traces of soap. The side of his ass cradled my cheek as I stuck my face down lower and lapped at his hole. Beauregard moaned and tried to spread his bound legs.

Nothing in all my life had turned me on more. I plunged my tongue downward and ate him out. No pretense, no restraint. I pushed my tongue deeper and deeper as he relaxed. Beau moaned with every wet thrust. We lost track of individual pleasure and simply floated in a sea of alternating satisfaction and desire.

At first Beau's hips arched, then they thrashed. His ass started to meet my tongue. Our breathing became a rhythmic moan of desperation for each other. As my own urges intensified, Beau's moans went from strained whispers to jagged whines. "Maria, I do not know what you are doing to me but…" He groaned and I flicked my tongue over the rim of his ass.

I arched up and led my finger over his hole. "Is this something you want?" His answer was to push his hips up to meet my hand. It was not enough. "Tell me, Please tell me Beau."

Maybe it wasn't mistress-like to ask, but I needed him by this point. His rough request nearly made me cum. "Maria. I need you. In every way."

I pushed my finger into his ass. The muscle instinctively tightened, then relaxed. I licked around it, partly to make sure the area stayed wet, partly, because it felt good and right in the moment. We played for a while that way. It felt good. It was fun. We both knew we needed more.

"Maria." Beauregard's voice was strained. His pleasure had been overshadowed by need and confusion. "I do not even…" His ragged moans cut off his words when I pushed my finger deeper. "I think you have changed me…"

Again he moaned. I relented. This was not the time to force detailed, sordid requests. "Beauregard Mathis, are you ready for me?"

At first he nodded, then seemed to remember words. "Yes."

I grabbed for lube as quickly as I could. My eager want was apparent, and I forced myself to be careful. After lubing the shaft between my legs, I used my fingers to tease it into Beau's hole. He moaned and bucked.

I grabbed my athamé from my bedside table and cut through the ropes as quickly as I could. I wanted him to buck. I wanted his moaning, writhing, fucking beautiful ass beneath me.

I grabbed Beau next. He willingly let me pull his hips up, and then down a bit so his ass matched my hips. Then I found myself holding my breath.

For all my release of inhibition, my hand was trembling as I led the phallus into my love. It wasn't smooth and perfect. Though I had chosen a small toy, it was Beauregard's first time. Too many emotions were involved for me and I slipped then had to steady myself.

We found ourselves laughing softly together. I heard my own nervousness in Beau's voice, and realized he had also needed to let go of trepidation to find himself here. I leaned forward to kiss his ass, and then pulled his hips gently back as I aligned myself better and entered him.

The half of the toy inside me tilted. It felt wonderfully connecting. Beau's hips tensed, then relaxed. We stayed like that at first, simply connected. Our more carnal desires engaged and we began to rock against one another.

At first it was a soft bounce. Beauregard seemed to be testing the sensation. I held tight to one hip and trailed fingers of my other hand in loving circles over his lower back. Beau arched his ass up and shoved back hard.

I pulled him in tighter, and then let him bounce away. He started to slide down my cock and I shoved it hard into him. We alternated, testing how to fuck each other in this new way. We soon found a tempo and countered thrusting and rocking.

It amazed me. The strongest person I knew was fucking himself against me. Part of me was in lust with pure sensation. Part of me was in awe. All of me needed more.

I gripped both his hips and started slamming him back. It seemed to undermine our rhythm, so I divided the force between pulling him back and thrusting forward. Beauregard instinctively joined in the motion, adding his own push back and moaning as I filled him.

It did not take long until I was at the brink of orgasm again. I surrendered to the delicious overflow of sensation. It gripped me tighter and held me longer than I was prepared for. I had to grip Beauregard's hips to keep from collapsing. As that strange pleasure washed over me, it drown out where we were and what was happening, leaving only bitter-sweet delights that bordered on painful in their intensity.

My cock slipped out as I sat back, and I pulled Beau onto my lap in a hazy embrace. His shoulders seemed massive compared to my smaller frame. Still, it felt good to hold him. For all the violent lovemaking, I hadn't thought about the reversal of simpler pleasures. Is this how he felt when he pulled me onto his lap? Strong, comforting, protective and possessive feelings accompanied the pose.

His back was solid and warm against my cheek. Many of the red marks had softened to a warm pink. Beauregard's breathing steadied from jagged gasping to a steady ebb and flow of air.

I thought of further steps, other delights or tortures I could introduce Beau to. They seemed suddenly superfluous in our sacred, quiet space. I thought of reassuring him, but knew he did not need empty or patronizing words.

Beau's head tilted toward mine. I kissed his cheek. Then I shifted so we could face each other. My lips sought his in a kiss that was a soft greeting. His return kiss was warm. I turned my back toward him. "Do you know how to loosen a corset?"

"It has been a while, but I am sure I can manage." His voice was tinged with humor. His hands were steady, and after some tugging and pulling I could slip my corset off.

The rest of my clothing soon followed. I led Beau to my shower and together, we relaxed under the rain.

LOVE

By Sumiko Saulson

Year 2: Alt-Alcatraz

They were best friends.

Maybe it was a natural thing for them to be close. X'ahsia learned a lot of what he knew about human emotion and how it worked by being inside Shane. That should have been enough, but he wanted more. Maybe it was more than he should want. X'ahsia wasn't human. He wasn't even humanoid. He was a collection of cooperative cells that could take any form it wished to. He was a swarm of microscopic drones that became cognizant, and without needing a queen bee, formed a hive mind. He was many tiny life forms acting in concert. Every single one of them loved Shane.

He loved Shane.

They were weeding the old warden's garden when he decided to tell his best friend that he was falling in love with him.

Shane was wearing a pair of faded gray leather gardening gloves with a blue and red line pattern nearly eroded from them. Frustrated by his inability to bleach or dye his hair, he'd given himself a Mohawk. X'ahsia was glad Shane had a Mohawk, because it meant he needed help to shave his head. He enjoyed grooming his friend. He appreciated any excuse for touching him. He liked the fact that they lived together, in the same house. Although they didn't share the same bed, they shared a bedroom. Two twin beds, one on either side of the room, like a dorm. X'ahsia often watched Shane sleeping. He was watching him gardening now.

X'ahsia was terrified. If Shane rejected his advances, he might decide to end their friendship. That would be unbearable. Still, there was a time to take chances, and that time had come. He leaned forward and touched the young human's hair with his three fingered hand. Each of the fingers ended in a gently rounded bulb, like a newt or a gecko. He ran the finger down a few loose strands of dark hair flying in the wind. He delicately smoothed it down on the side of Shane's face. He stopped for a moment and let his fingers linger on the young man's cheek for a minute, then let go.

Shane chuckled nervously. "Hey, what are you doing? Stop messing around. We're here to work."

Shane thought his strange alien friend might be hitting on him, but he wasn't sure. He was almost twenty, but he had almost no experience with such things. He was a fat kid when he came here. He wasn't exactly attracting the women. He'd lost the weight and put on some muscle since then, but there weren't exactly a wide range of potential love interests on Alternate Alcatraz. The closest woman to his age was a lesbian. The only other woman was old enough to be his grandmother and in a relationship. Both of the other dudes were very old and very straight. Was he straight? Right now, he didn't know. He thought maybe X'ahsia was hitting on him, or maybe he was just imagining things. He decided to ignore it for now. He went back to tilling the soil with a hand-held mini-hoe.

Only a few minutes passed before X'ahsia tapped him on the shoulder to get his attention. "What now?" Shane groaned.

"Have you seen the way Gerald and Rosalind work together?" X'ahsia probed.

The extraterrestrial had developed adaptive coloring lately, like a chameleon. It added to his mystery and altogether foreign appearance. Leaning against the fresh basil, his skin's cast went mottled green. He was giving Shane his best sincere puppy dog look. X'ahsia's eyes were large, ovular orbs that tipped up on the exterior edges. They were pure gold with flecks of bright shining metallic particles. He looked exactly the way Doreen drew him, but he didn't sound like her anymore. His voice was noncommittally gendered, somewhere between a high pitched male voice and a deeper female one.

"Of course I have," Shane acquiesced. "But that's different. They're lovers."

Everyone knew about Gerry and Rosie. There was a twenty-seven year age difference between them. If they were still back in the regular timeline – which Shane presumed still existed – Rosalind's children and grandchildren would have been quite scandalized by a respectable sixtyish woman gallivanting around town with a thirty-something homeless white boy.

Well, no. Actually, lots of Filipina girls had white husbands in the Bay Area and they probably wouldn't care about the race. But the age difference was notable. He imagined people calling Rosie a cougar and Gerry a boy toy, and began to snicker. Gerry seemed far too old to be called a boy, toy or otherwise. But there were only seven people on the island – Rosie, Gerry, Margo, Mark, Maurice, X'ahsia and himself. Sometimes it got really lonely. Shane was glad Rosie and Gerry had each other.

"What are lovers?" X'ahsia asked with feigned innocence. He knew.

"They give pleasure to each other," Shane explained bashfully.

"How?" X'ahsia coyly proceeded.

"With their bodies," Shane said, feeling a little hot with embarrassment and mildly aroused by this turn in the conversation. "They touch each other's bodies." He gave X'ahsia a funny look. This alien was definitely hitting on him. He'd never had anyone show sexual interest in him before. It was strangely intoxicating. He wondered if X'ahsia might want to touch his body.

"It's getting hot," Shane said calculatedly. "I've got to get out of this shirt." He began slowly peeling his shirt off, watching the alien to see how he reacted. The golden flecks in X'ahsia's eyes usually drifted aimlessly. Now they began to move in an agitated manner. The creature's green skin gradually resumed its original lavender tint, which made it look like he was blushing. Shane noticed that X'ahsia was breathing heavily. That was particularly conspicuous because the alien didn't actually need to breathe.

Shane quickly pulled his shirt down and laughed.

"Oh my God! You're totally into me!" he shrieked excitedly. He jumped up and down. He thought that was awesome, and he was never going to let X'ahsia live it down. He leaned down, gave the lavender man a big bear hug and then let go and fell back on the ground laughing.

"Come on now, you can tell me. You want this, don't you?" Shane gestured towards himself with both thumbs. "I mean this. This is what you like, right?" He was gloating a little. He pulled his shirt off and smirked at X'ahsia, who was looking slightly uncomfortable.

Shane playfully curled his arm and made a muscle. "You definitely think I'm hot."

X'ahsia shook his head. "I do like you, but you don't have to be so immature about it. I don't just mean I want you physically. I mean I love you. I learned everything about love by being inside you."

Shane stopped laughing and suddenly grew very quiet.

"Did I say something wrong?" X'ahsia asked, pouting a little. He wanted to reach out and touch Shane, but he was afraid to. They both sat there in silence for some time. After a few minutes, Shane took his gloves off and took one of X'ahsia's hands in both of his.

"Listen," he said gently, "it's okay that you like me that way. I don't know how I feel about that. I've never really thought about it before. I mean Rosie and Gerry are one thing, they are different ages and different races, but like – it's like I'm a nineteen year old Chinese guy and you're like a four thousand year old alien and shit. We aren't the same species and the age difference is outrageous. And wow. You're not even one alien, are you?"

"No, I'm not, we are many, but we are of one mind, and all of us love you." X'ahsia pled. He could feel the rejection coming, and started to tremble.

"Don't get all emotional and shit," Shane said gruffly. Something about this kind of attention filled him with a need for macho posturing. All that nineteen year old machismo kicked in. "I didn't say no, I just said I need some time to think about it. It never occurred to me that you might be, like uhm, sexual. I mean for fuck's sake, you don't even have genitals."

"I could make myself form genitals," X'ahsia offered.

"Yikes! That's too far, can we… not go there right now?" Shane protested, dropping the alien's hand. He shook his head. "I haven't been with anyone and you're going too fast."

"I haven't been with anyone either," X'ahsia claimed. Of course, that wasn't entirely accurate. He was constantly reproducing asexually. Cells of X'ahsia were splitting and other ones were dying on a daily basis. He hadn't been with anyone sexually, though. He supposed that the Others could sexually reproduce – after all, there was Angela and Nathaniel. He wanted to find out how it was done, experiment a little.

"If I made female genitals, do you think we could reproduce sexually?" X'ahsia blurted out. Shane held his head in his hands and groaned. To him, X'ahsia acted like a love-struck teenage girl. It was a lot to deal with.

"I just need you to listen to me and try not to talk," Shane said uncomfortably. "When you talk about this, it just gives me a headache. I don't want to reproduce with you or anyone, X'ahsia. First of all, I'm only nineteen. That means I'm like, barely an adult. Maybe when I'm old, like Gerry or something, I might change my mind. Second of all, we're trapped on an island in a pocket of time during a probable pre-apocalypse. I think it would be very irresponsible to have children under these circumstances.

"I also need you to understand that even though you have very pleasant memories of possessing my body, my memories of it are not pleasant at all. I don't like it when you talk about being inside me. You hurt me when you possessed me, X'ahsia. So if you really do love me, you need to promise me that you'll never do that to me again."

"I promise I will never hurt you again," X'ahsia said sincerely. The alien was beginning to cry. Red-tinged tears slid out of its brilliant yellow eyes and down its violet cheeks. Shane felt bad for it… for him. There was no sense pretending he wasn't talking to another guy. Still, he quietly pulled his shirt off and used it to dry X'ahsia's tears as if the thousands of year old space invader were a fifteen year old girl with a painful crush. A girl he liked as a friend, but not romantically. A girl who desired him, and he enjoyed being wanted.

"We could be here forever," Shane said unhappily. "I'm not trying to be mean about it because I know you have feelings for me. But what if I don't feel the same way, but I just don't want to be alone?" He shivered at the cold truth of it. "Would you still sleep with me? I mean like uhm… a friend with benefits, or something?"

"You don't have to be alone," X'ahsia reassured him. "We can be or not be whatever you want us to be. You are the one in control of our relationship.

I'll take my cues from you. We won't do anything you don't want to."

"Thanks," Shane said, leaning back against his hands. "I would feel a lot more comfortable about it that way. But uhm, yea. I thought about it. It might be kind of cool. Like Captain Kirk, he got all the hot green alien chicks on Star Trek. But you're not a chick, are you?"

"Technically speaking, I'm genderless," X'ahsia admitted. "I can be a man or a woman or neither. I can be a woman for you if you need me to be."

"That would be hella fake. You still wouldn't be a woman," Shane frowned. "You'd be a guy pretending to be a woman so his boyfriend could pretend to be straight. Which would be kind of bullshit, so much so as that I want to say, I don't want you to have change your gender because of me. That's just fucked up." Shane was getting upset and babbling a little.

X'ahsia grinned at the word "boyfriend" but didn't say anything.

"I'm also pretending to be a man," he said carefully. "I don't actually have any gender. I prefer being a man to being a woman but… I only call myself 'he' because I don't like 'it.' Either way, like you say, I'm an asexually reproducing conglomerate of organisms playing at being gendered. I'm technically agender."

Shane shrugged. "Fuck this conversation. You don't have to decide what your gender is today, and I don't have to decide what the nature of our relationship can be. It's just that you say you love me, and I'm happy about that. I'm really nervous I'm… not sure what to say. But I thought I would live and die without anyone wanting to be with me that way, so I'm more than just flattered, I'm grateful."

He gave his friend a clumsy hug, and they went back to gardening like nothing ever happened. When they went home that night, they mutually decided to push their twin beds together in the center of the room and try just sleeping together. No touching, just sleeping.

Several days went by before they decided it would be warmer if they also slept under the same blankets. They were both still in pajamas, but they innocently hugged under the blankets the way the post-sexual and pre-sexual do. Like an ancient married couple whose sex life went the way of the dodo long ago, or a couple of preteen girls on a sleepover.

Shane apologized for snoring but X'ahsia said he didn't mind.

For a while, it seemed as if they would just leave things at this platonic level of affection indefinitely. Two weeks later, when they finally kissed, it took X'ahsia by surprise. Shane was wearing garish black and white striped faux prison garment from the gift shop. X'ahsia was snuggled up close in an equally tacky gray "Property of Alcatraz" t-shirt. His form was petite in comparison to Shane's. He was a head shorter and his arms and legs were almost comically thin. The t-shirt he wore was an XXXL that hung down to his knees like a nightgown.

Shane bent his down and pressed his mouth against X'ahsia's tentatively.

He gave him a series of soft, gentle kisses, tender and sweet with no tongue. They were innocent first kisses. The alien smiled and returned them in kind.

"I've never kissed anyone," Shane explained. "No one except my mom and grandma is what I am trying to say. I mean I've never kissed a girl or a boy even. Or you like this."

Shane kissed him again, slowly and passionately. With every kiss his desire increased. Soon, he was sucking and biting X'ahsia's lower lip. He thrust his tongue between the alien's lips until they parted. X'ahsia met the kisses trembling with unfulfilled desire. He wanted to take things much further, but he had told Shane they could go at his pace.

And then, because he had been told he was in charge of this thing between them, Shane gave in to his own overwhelming need to assert his masculinity. He threw X'ahsia on his back leaned on top of him. He began fondle his delicate, genderless body. What he found under the baggy shirt astounded him. The alien's chest was as plain and featureless as a human's back was. He had no nipples and no belly button, just an expanse of smooth, supple skin. The soft mound between X'ahsia's legs was as barren and empty as a Ken doll's crotch. It was freaky.

Shane gently lowered the t-shirt and covered his would-be lover.

"I really don't know what I'm doing here," Shane apologized.

"I like it, whatever it is," X'ahsia said. He pulled his shirt off and tossed it aside. "I like the way it feels when your skin touches my skin. I want all to rub all of my flesh against yours. I want my fingers to touch all of you."

Shane ran his hands down his companion's back and cradled his equally featureless rear end. The alien didn't have a single organ for sexual reproduction, urination, or defecation. X'ahsia was like a warm, fleshy doll. But his skin was so soft.

"You're a really good kisser," Shane said thoughtfully. "I like kissing you." He kissed the alien again just to make sure X'ahsia knew he was sincere. Then he continued his speech.

"The thing is, I think that you're missing a lot of uhm, parts, though. Like most of the ones humans usually use for sex. And it's weird for me, touching you sexually like this and finding nothing there to, err, make love with."

He put his arms around X'ahsia's waist and resumed kissing him. It was far more fulfilling than pretending to kiss someone else while sucking the crook of his own arm. He ran his hands over the silky, pale lavender skin. Tomorrow was Shane's birthday and he didn't really want to be a twenty year old virgin. His willing playmate didn't seem to have the equipment for fucking, so this kind of intimacy would have to do.

"I have fingers, and a mouth," X'ahsia reminded him. "And whatever parts you have, I can stroke them, I can kiss them. Just show them to me and help me understand what is required to please you. Does that sound good?"

"I'm not sure," Shane said. He was already undressing because it sounded very good. He started to imagine what it would feel like to have those kisses travel down from his mouth to other places on his body.

"It's probably a good idea," he quickly amended. "We could spend the rest of our lives here. I mean I could get old and die here an old wrinkled virgin, and I don't want that." When he was completely naked, he pulled X'ahsia against him so he could feel the warmth of skin against skin. X'ahsia's hands were quickly upon him, searching for and finding all of the ways in which a human body was different from his own.

When Shane let go, he fell back into his pillows and swore a little. No matter what protests his mouth made, his body betrayed his desire. His pulse was racing and his dick was hard. He wanted his body thoroughly explored by X'ahsia's curious fingers and hungry mouth.

"Shit! Well okay then," Shane muttered. "You can kiss me down there."

He involuntarily shuttered as his mouth formed the words. Shane wasn't sure how this would give X'ahsia gratification and he didn't care. He was filled with a longing to receive carnal pleasure selfishly. To have his friend who loved him, licking and sucking him in secret places no one else had touched. X'ahsia didn't wait for a second invitation. He buried his head between Shane's legs and tenderly delivered the birthday gift he knew his beloved human friend desperately craved.

In doing so, he took something away for himself. X'ahsia extracted his dear one's genetic material in the most natural and affectionate way possible. One day this beautiful human he adored would grow old and die. X'ahsia didn't want to be alone. He stored Shane's genetic material. Someday, if they were both ready… or in the terrible event that Shane's life came to an end, they might have a child.

BIMBO SUTRA #2

By Skunkheart

Disclaimer: *This poem is fifteen years and was my first attempt to understand my bimbo fetish.*

Instinct lurks beneath the water-strong surface of her words.
Somewhere,
a beat,
loud,
slow,
and savage.
A giggle skip-echoes across time. The bimbo
has arrived, and I am jealous of her animalistic enlightenment.
Everything returns to normal speed as her bubble-gum entrance
ends.
That sourceless beat becomes just another mindless pop song again and
she is standing there by the door,
nature pink in lip and claw,
while I am sitting here across the floor,
watching her through an ever-moving jungle
of dancing bodies
as she grants muscled arm the bestial grace of glittery fingernails
and a coy cock of her head.

Hehe.

His attention is all she wants,
and she is single-mindedly hunting it down
like some fucked-up deer stalks down a lion just to get eaten by it,
because, later on,

he will sink fleshy fang into the meat beneath her stomach, a part of their one-night relationship
which,
truth be told, she's not entirely fond of,
but at least she knows that for a few scant hours,
the only thing on his mind was
her. Like any Buddhist,
the bimbo asserts her own unique self through its destruction.

She is history turned back in upon itself in an ouroboros circle.
Those primal thoughtless wordless days of four ends in life –
eating,
shitting,
fucking,
and dying –
gone through endless perturbations of civilization. From
Egypt with its eternities to the United States and its freedoms,
it all comes back down
to this:
the bimbo,
a blessedly human creature with four perfect purposes in life:
to eat,
to shit,
to get fucked,
and to die. It's
not that women are submissive,
but that they can be,
and like any Muslim, the bimbo understands that submission is sacred.

There is a nirvana to be found here,
as she buries her memories
and becomes a new person
with each beat of her heart,
because man
invented reason so that he
might see an alien and unknowable god,
but like any child the bimbo knows that there is only
one thing in this world worth our worship:

the world itself.

And she
is its priestess and she

is its monk,
and her scriptures are her blood
and the pumping of her partner
and her prayers are every drink
and every brush of make-up across her perfect skin,
and when she kneels before him,
head bobbing like the hand of a hip-hop monk listening to a truly dope Gregorian chant-rap,
it is not
the re-enactment of some patriarchal power fantasy. No,
she is kneeling at her altar,
seeking an ecstasy unmatched by any of the transcendental
religions in which she was raised.

I am
not yet familiar with these mysteries.
I am still just an acolyte,
a virgin,
a porn addict who hopes with fanatic hope
that the weak feeling in my knees that comes when I shove holy scepter
into my tabernacle
will lead me down the aisle like the bishop
in his phallic miter and
staff to my First
Communion.

OREOS

By Lif

"I don't get it," Shelly said, craning her neck to either side to stretch her muscles. "How did they know which window he was shooting from? I can't see a thing in any of the windows from the street-level shots."

"The whole scene is tinted darker," Aaron said "to show the mood."

"I thought you said the whole point the director had in mind was sight," Shelly argued, "to emulate as much of what each character could see in the moment, as possible."

Aaron paused, his hand frozen over the Oreo bowl for a moment before answering. This hesitation was not lost on Shelly, who was already grinning.

"They could have followed the trajectory-"

"No way could they follow it that accurately in the moment, from the ground!"

"-and/or then seen the flashes from the gun when looking in the general direction."

"That's weak," Shelly said, "but let's go with that - why are they shooting at a tenth-story window from the ground, with pistols, instead of clearing the area and locking down the building until they have backup to go in?"

"Because you're too fucking smart, that's why!" Aaron mock-shouted, as Shelly rolled back laughing.

"You think it's funny?" he asked. He paused the movie and picked up the bowl of Oreos to move it aside.

The simple action was a clear signal to Shelly of what was coming. Her laughter almost died on her lips, a nervous chuckle the only remnants as she clutched her pillow tightly to her body, eyes wide and locked on her Master as he leaned forward.

"You think it's amusing," he continued, "that you're being so smart without permission?"

"No, Sir." The reply was instinctual, and came on a timid, breathy whisper. Gone was the audacious, cheeky mirth. Now, she was a deer in his headlights.

"Not at all," he told her. "Remind me - what makes a good girl?"

"Dumb and obedient?"

Aaron smiled, and tapped her on the nose. "Dumb...obedient...and *wet.*"

Shelly bit her lip at the last word, and failed to keep her legs still as they squeezed together. There was something about his hands that had always driven her wild, no matter where they touched her. Something about them had always been so alive - strong, and flexible, with an occasional callous and bit of scarring from crafting.

"Is my girl wet?" he asked. "I've already caught you thinking...perhaps I need to check in."

His fingers snaked their way in between the pillow and her belly. She planned to make him work for it, but the feel of his touch already rendered her powerless to hold on to the pillow as it fell away from her, his hand slipping under the waistband of her sweatpants and his index finger finding its mark against her panties. Was she wet? Within seconds of his touch, the answer quickly became a yes, just as they both knew it would.

"There's my girl," he cooed, his eyes shining as he felt his work, gently running his finger along the shape of her slit through her panties. "Wetter and dumber."

"Wetter and dumber," she whispered, feeling it become so in her mind. Every move of his finger against her sex was mirrored by his words against her mind. She felt herself switching off, and melting into his voice.

"You want these off?" he asked, flicking the waistband of her sweats with his thumb.

She nodded her breaths heavy and open-mouthed as she began to thrust into the movements of his hand.

"Say it," he hissed.

"Yes Sir! I want them off. Please."

He withdrew his hand as she mewled in dismay. "Take them off," he commanded her. Give me a show."

Shelly both loved and hated when he gave that order. She always felt so out of her depth, and clueless as to what to do. Even so, no matter what she chose to do, the feeling of being forced to do it for his enjoyment was always worth the humiliation. She stood, swaying her hips slowly as she worked the waistband down past her hips to her thighs, showing off the wet stain on her panties, as she thrust it towards him.

"Yours," she whispered, as she slipped the pants down another several inches, finally giving a firm shake of herself to drop them to her ankles...only the pants did not fall. Even when she shook a second time. She was mortified. But bless him, despite his obvious amusement; he did not make a sound. She saved herself as best she could, using her thumbs to push the pants down, and kicking them away, squatting down and spreading her legs to offer him what was rightfully his.

"Look at that," he said, grinning as he watched her wetness shine, and drip from between her legs. “We are making progress. Do you want to touch?” His voice was like syrup. She wanted to drown in it. As long as she could listen to him, nothing else could ever matter.

“Yes Sir, please!” Her hips were making the smallest of thrusts, outside of her control. “Let me touch, let me touch, please Sir, let me touch!”

He leaned closer, inhaling her scent with a smirk. The sight of that smirk made Shelly shake even more violently. “You may,” he told her.

Within an instant, her hand flew to her sex, touching herself with two fingers, one on either side of her clit. She gently dragged her hand up; brushing her clit from either side, mewling as she again bucked her hips. She repeated the motion several more times before allowing her fingertips to begin circling against her clit, biting her lips as she drew closer to climax.

Aaron watched with delight as she neared her orgasm, studying the motions of her body as her muscles tightened, and her cries grew higher. “That sounds to me like someone’s getting close,” he murmured. “But I don’t recall saying you were allowed to come, yet.”

Shelly whined in dismay, less than a minute away from orgasm but obediently slowing her motions to keep herself safely away from the point of no return. “Please,” she groaned. “Please let me come.”

“I don't think so,” he crowed, feasting on her frustration. "I don't think you're quite dumb enough, just yet.”

“You're right. Make me dumber,” she begged. “Please Sir. Make me dumb, make me wet, and keep me there.”

“And what do you need,” Aaron asked, “to stay in your rightful state?”

“You,” she breathed. “In me, please. I should never cum without being used for your pleasure, I'm too dumb. Make use of me as I should be used. Please!”

Aaron was already climbing to his feet to step towards her when by the worst of luck, his foot landed on the edge of the Oreo bowl. The cookies were catapulted into the air, scattering this way and that. Most were sent across the bed. Several nicked the wall or the floor, sending the cat scurrying out the door. One perfectly fearless Oreo, however, landed square in between Shelly’s eyes before landing directly on her panties, over the wet spot.

Aaron burst out laughing, sinking down to his knees to hug his even more mortified girl, and draw her in for a kiss. “Oh, fuck, sorry babe!”

Just like that, the world dropped out from under Shelly. In an instant, the bed was gone. So were the Oreos, the movie, the cat, and Aaron - and with them, everything that had come to make Shelly herself in the last two years.

Suddenly, she was in a different and much dirtier bedroom. She was naked, laying with her face turned towards the wall, too numb to even pull the covers over herself as another man sat at the edge of the bed, glancing back at her on occasion before breaking the silence. “Sorry babe,” Jackson said, “I should have actually asked first. You know, I just assumed because we always...you know, it's been a week. And you didn't exactly say *no,* you know…"

Or else, they were in the bathroom, Shelly holding him and rubbing his back through his shirt as he vomited into the toilet. "Sorry babe," he choked out in between heaves. "I thought I could handle a few more. This isn't-" he paused to retch - "This isn't normal. I can usually handle myself. You'll tell your folks that, right?"

Or they were in the kitchen, as she washed off the wound on her arm, the warm soap suds burning her as they ran pink into the sink, all while he watched from where he sat in the corner. "Sorry babe, it was a total accident. I didn't mean to go off like that, I just wasn't thinking. You know that, yeah?"

Or she was sobbing in the car, parked around the corner, freezing cold even with the heat blasting, knowing that she could not stay there forever, she had to go back inside at some point, thumbing open her phone to see his new message: "Babe, I'm sorry, I wasn't thinking. You know I didn't mean a word of that. I love you, and this isn't me, this is just my shit talking." The words were almost worth believing, and she dared not scroll up to the messages from the past hour beforehand.

She was in none of these situations, of course. She had not been for years, and yet it had all come back so clearly, so vividly. She wished that she could say it passed as quickly as it came, but it did not. Now, she was living in a double exposure - safe in Aaron's arms at the same time that she was convincing herself that she was safe in Jackson's.

"I'm sorry," Aaron was whispering, "I'm so sorry, Shelly. I forgot that word, and what it meant."

"It's okay," she said, tearing herself out of the fog in her head as best she knew how. "It's not your fault."

"What can I do?" he asked.

"I don't know," she said, the only words that were coming. Try as she might, she could not entirely shake herself free of the fog, and found that she was already clutching the pillow against her body again, now for very different reasons. It was bad enough that she had ruined the scene, but now seeing Aaron's helplessness in his face made it even worse. They had been having so much fun and now one stupid ass word from him had pulled it all apart.

Of course, if she had the clarity to voice all of this, he would disagree. He would tell her it was natural, that she had not ruined anything, but even that truth was so...empty, and barely visible through the fog in her head. She became aware that he was still speaking, and wrenched her attention back to him, trying to ignore how...unclean, she suddenly felt with sweat on her skin and other wetness between her legs.

"Do you want to watch more of the movie?" he was asking, "or something to drink?"

Both of these sounded lovely, and yet completely irrelevant at the same time. "I don't know," she felt herself repeating, and cursed herself for it. Like a stupid, broken record.

She heard his intake of breath, and felt his arms wrap even tighter around her.

"How about," he asked, "we just do nothing, for a bit? We don't even have to talk. Let's just stay here like this, for as long as you need, mkay?"

It was as good an answer as any - and in fact, better than anything else specific. Something about not having to decide gave her another drop of relief from the fog, and her pounding heart. She nodded, and they remained in silence for several long moments as he kept her wrapped in his arms, and she kept the pillow wrapped in her own, before she finally spoke - albeit into the pillow: "...do we still have any Oreos?"

THE CLEARING

By Ouroboros Sings

Part I

They had arrived late the night before—Master, slave, and Pet—with just enough energy to pitch tent and then retire, naked and snuggled together in their three bags zipped together as one, drifting to sleep in one another's warmth and beating hearts.

Pet awoke with a start to the screech of Stellar's jay, to find herself alone—Master and slave must have gone for a stroll. With a big yawn, she stumbled out of the tent to the picnic table, grabbed a mug and the coffee pot—still warm enough to drink; they couldn't have been away for long. The sun shone through the bay laurel, filling the air with heady scent; its dappled light dancing upon her bare skin. A gentle breeze raised goosebumps and caused her nipples to perk up.

Her ears perked up—a snapping twig. She turned toward the sound...

No, not a deer: Master walked towards her holding a freshly cut, green branch and sporting a length of rope coiled diagonally across his shoulder. With his leather cowboy hat, denim, and boots, he looked quite like a dashing, and rather more-sophisticated, Indiana Jones...

"My pet, finish your coffee and come with me."

Pet set down her cup and started for the tent. "That won't be necessary," he interrupted, "I have your clothes right here." He pulled the collar and leash from his back pocket. "Come here, girl." Pet scampered up to Master and knelt before him. "Good girl," he praised her as he buckled on the leather collar and checked it for fit, "we're going for a nice walk now. Come on!"

They left camp, Master leading his Pet into the woods. Feeling so naked and vulnerable, Pet grew keenly aware of her surroundings: a dragonfly buzzed her head, curious at the site of such an incongruous animal; Madrone branches rubbed against groaning redwoods, invoking thoughts of arms and legs entwined; the babbling creek made her aware of the fullness in her bladder.

"Oh Master?" "Yes, my pet?" "I must relieve myself." "Of course, my pet. Why don't you stand there, in the sunlight and let your Master watch you?" Doing as she was told, Master's Pet widened her stance, reached between her legs, and with her fingers parted her slick labia. At first, she blushed and hesitated, being watched like this, but eventually the yellow liquid streamed out, catching the sunlight like molten gold; the sound of its splatter mimicking the nearby water. She stepped to the edge of the creek, squatted, and splashed herself with ice-cold water, both shocking and a relief. Sparked by the urge to play with herself, she reached down and plunged her fingers deep into her well.

"No!" The jerk of the leash was just hard enough to throw her to her knees. "Bad girl! Did I give you permission to do that?" Pet kowtowed to her Master, kissed the instep of his boot.

The momentary pause brought to Pet's attention the fact that Master's slave was nowhere to be seen. She wondered where that lass could be, but sensed this was not a question to ask.

"Come, now." They strolled just a short way further; Master stopped and surveyed the scene. "Yes, this will do nicely. Here—stand right here." Master directed Pet between two young-but-sturdy redwoods. "Now, give me your hand." He took her by the wrist and tied on one end of the rope; looping the gathered coils around one tree, crossing it over her chest, around the other tree, around her other wrist, back and forth, ankles too. Quickly, carefully, and deftly, Master secured Pet in such a manner as to spread her arms and legs wide, leaving her just barely enough to balance and keep herself upright.

The vulnerability Pet had been feeling along the walk was nothing compared to how she now felt, so exposed and helpless.

"There, now you can't run away," Master grinned, and kissed and caressed his Pet; he ran his fingers through her hair, along her arms, down her haunches. He walked behind her and traced down her spine, rubbed and kneaded her ass. Pressing his body against her, he reached around front and grabbed her breasts, pulling her tight against him; his belt buckle dug into the small of her back. She gasped. "Such a bad girl, my pet." Master kissed and nibbled the back of Pet's neck, and rolled her hardened nipples twixt his thumb and finger; Pet groaned with pleasure, a swelling warmth rising between her legs. The Master pinched—pinched hard—*very* hard. Pet cried out! The Stellar's jays scattered. Pinching gave way to gentle, soothing caresses… then another pinch—oh, she cried! It hurt so, and yet—oh, the pleasure! Master reached down and felt between her legs—so wet, like heavy dew, she was. "Not quite ready," Master thought out loud.

He eased off, stepped back, and stood quietly behind his Pet. Her heart raced in anticipation. "Where is Master's slave?" she silently wondered, "why isn't she here, with me?" Something brushed lightly against her skin—what? So many fingers—what was it? Up her legs, across her bottom, along her back again; it felt cool, sometimes soft, sometimes scratch…ing…—ah, the willow branch.

Then nothing.

Swoosh! The sting against her bottom caused her to yelp. More sharp swings of the branch across the back of her thighs. Master continued to flog Pet, his voice in rhythmic beat to his swings: "you must…understand…being…a new pet…means you need…to be disciplined. We cannot…have you running…wild." The willow branch repeatedly stung her back, her arms, her ass, and her thighs.

Then nothing again.

Then footsteps walking away, a splash in the creek; footsteps returning, the feel of soothing, ice-cold water poured down her back. Oh god, such relief! Master walked around and stood facing his Pet, who looked up at her Master, weakly but adoringly, with tear-streaked cheeks. "There, there, my pet—your Master is not angry with you; you are a very good girl, you simply require more training." Master kissed her deeply as one hand roamed down again between her legs to check for wetness.

"There, *now* you are ready. And I have a present for you!"

Part II

Master untied his now very-weakened Pet and held her in his arms. "Are you alright, my little pet?" he whispered. She nodded her head, "mm-hmmm," she replied in a long, low hum. She enjoyed this moment, feeling Master's body, strong and lithe, his member hard, twitching. "Come now. Your pain shall be rewarded."

Master took up the leash and led his Pet to a clearing in the woods, whereupon Pet gasped: before her eyes, an Angel was laid prone with arms and legs spread wide, secured by satin sashes tied to pegs hammered into the ground. She glowed in the brilliant ray of sun piercing through the trees—she was of alabaster so fair and white that it gave Pet cause to squint. It was only then that she noticed the decorations etched into the surface of the Angel's skin, colorful drawings mingling with the grass caressing this lovely apparition.

The Angel smiled, offering a smiling invitation. Pet turned to Master, with desire and begging in her wide eyes; Master nodded his assent, and guided her toward the Angel. Pet stood motionless, her heart still pounding from surprise and rising lust. She knelt down alongside the Angel, brushed her fingers through the golden silk hair, caressed the delicate skin; she swirled her fingers around the Angel's hardening nipples, and took one firmly between her finger and thumb—the Angel froze—the Pet wanted to squeeze it, squeeze it hard—but the thought of making this Angel cry? Would Master approve? She released the cherry; the Angel exhaled.

Oh, how Pet felt agitated by this denial of pleasure—her own pleasure! Keenly aware of the pulsing ache in her groin, compulsion overtook her: she quickly undid the sashes around the Angel's ankles, then flipped around and sat down, pressing her vulva hard on the Angel's face; then leaned over, reached under the Angel's thighs and hoisted up her legs, bringing her knees down onto her chest, spreading her thighs wide open, fully exposing her flower… and… then…

Pet froze…

At that moment, the sun seemed to narrow its beam to focus upon this succulent fruit; its nectar glistened on tender folds of skin surrounding a pink pearl. A grassy, musky aroma rose from within. It was such a vision… This delicate, juicy Angel's fruit… so pink, so swollen…

And yet…

Pet could wait no further—she drove her face into the moist flesh and hungrily devoured it: her tongue swirled and caressed the labia, her teeth nibbled—sometimes sharply—the hood, the clit; she pressed and rolled her face in this juicy dessert as she pressed and rolled her pelvis against the Angel's face. Muffled protests turned to muffled groans of ecstasy; the Angel kicked her legs and squeezed Pet's hips with her thighs, her body shook and arched in violent pleasure. Pet continued to suck and lick; she growled with passion, savoring the delicious meal. Finally, the sound of a muffled squeal from between her thighs; another shudder, and the Angel fell limp, but for her heaving chest and just the barest hint of a smile.

Pet's hunger was satisfied, but her lust remained. She turned and laid herself down on the still-quaking body of the Angel, and kissed her deeply, aroused by the taste of her own nectar on those ethereal lips. She cupped the Angel's breasts and sucked upon tender nipples, rolling the ball with her tongue, delicately tugging at the metal bar with her teeth—the Angel whimpered. This made Pet hungrier still and so she bit into the cherry…

A shriek. And then, a hand lay upon Pet's back. "There, girl, be still a moment," instructed Master. His obedient Pet remained still, on her knees, straddling the Angel; she pursed her lips and blew cool air on the tender, sore nipple.

Master knelt down behind his Pet, and reached through her legs for the Angel's vulva, brushing his arm against that of his Pet's as he worked his fingers between the Angel's petals and into her slit. "My dear Heavenly apparition, it is time I bring you down from On High…" and with that,

Master pierced his engorged cock into the Angel's cave—she cried out loud; birds took hasty flight. Placing both hands firmly on the shoulders of Pet, he pressed her body down onto the Angel's; thus using Pet as an anchor, as he rammed his great root into his Angel's hot, slippery hole. Wrapping his arms around both women and holding them tight, the Master slammed his hips over and over into the crying, smiling Angel as he bit his teeth into the shoulder of his Pet, thrusting and thrusting until he exploded in excruciating ecstasy.

The three collapsed to their sides, panting and sweaty. Pet reached up and released the fallen Angel's wrist restraints; slave, in turn, wrapped her wings around Master and Pet, and together they drifted into a dreamy state…

As the sun rose higher in the sky, the trio stirred; to head back to camp. On the return, the Master noted his Pet looking somewhat perturbed. "Why the frown, little one?" "Oh, Master," Pet meekly smiled, "I do not wish to suggest that what took place was anything less than wonderful…" "And yet…?" "I am ashamed to say."

Master and slave exchanged glances. "My pet, between us we have no shame," he declared. "You must feel free to speak your mind." This made Pet smile. "Then I shall tell you, Master: my body—my body still aches to be brought to… to…" She blushed, "dear Master, I have yet to be… fully pleasured, myself…"

Master and slave grinned at one another. "My dear pet, the day is young! After lunch, we have more in store. Do you know about the waterfall?"

"There's a waterfall…?" Pet looked at slave, who in turn blushed. They picked up the pace back to camp.

Part III

By the time they arrived at the cabin, an afternoon breeze had picked up, giving Pet and slave goosebumps, so Master allowed them to dress. "But neither of you are to wear your bras"—Master enjoyed seeing his charges' nipples poking through their soft T-shirts. (Truth be told, all three enjoyed the sight!)

Pet, who was tasked with all the cooking, set to making lunch. Anticipating further activities would surely follow—the sort where a heavy meal would interfere—she kept it light: pasta salad with chunks of red bell pepper, green olives, and many other delightful veggies lending color and nutrition, with a crumble of feta cheese, served with a bottle of crisp, dry white wine that had been kept chilled in the creek. Pet's belly warmed at the sight of Master and slave thoroughly relishing her fare.

Whilst slave cleaned up, Pet fed cherries to Master. Savoring their sweet, dark juice, Master reached over and dipped his hand into the V-neckline of Pet's shirt, lifting and exposing one of her pendulous breasts. With his other hand, he held a cherry to Pets lips and allowed her to bite into the fruit—Pet savored the treat—he then rubbed the half-cherry around her breast, staining the areola and nipple with red juice. Momentarily cupping this now-marked breast, Master enjoyed the feel of its bouncy weight in his hand; he pinched the nipple, and tucked the soft breast back inside Pet's T-shirt.

Finished with the dishes, slave bounced up alongside Pet, a ready look on her face. Pet picked up on the clue, and now both women, holding one another's hands, looked at Master with bright-eyed anticipation. "Alright, girls, I suppose it's time we were off," and with that Master clipped on their leashes, hoisted his satchel on his shoulder, and they made off for the waterfall.

The forest was filled with birdsong and the scent of dusty bay and fir. Insects busily buzzed, trees groaned. The banks of the creek grew steeper, high enough to create something of a modest little canyon. The babbling waters were gradually met by another sound: at first almost undetectable, the splash of a small waterfall grew more and more apparent, like wind through leaves—were it not that the afternoon air was so still. Just around the third bend of the creek, Master and his girls came upon a swimming hole; neither too large nor too small, it was deep enough for swimming yet also provided big, shallow areas where the granite refused to yield to centuries of water erosion. The waterfall, itself, was not much wider than one's shoulders; it arched gently away from the rocky cliff edge and hit the pond with a delicious splash.

In other words, this naturally formed pool offered a variety of play areas.

"Slave, why don't you take off your shoes and pants and go for a swim? ... No, I didn't say you could remove your shirt, now did I?"

Slave stood at the pond's edge, naked but for her T-shirt. Master and Pet delighted in this vision of a vulnerable forest nymph, the sun shimmering in liquid reflections upon her pale skin. Slave touched her toes to the water and instantly her nipples stiffened. The water felt cold, but not terribly uncomfortable, so she slowly moved in deeper, up to her knees, and then squatted. The feel of cool, clear water on her exposed pussy excited slave; she spread her legs further to let the water lap against her clit and anus; the look on her face was pure joy. Her areolas showed through her shirt, now made translucent by the waterfall's spray. Slave became aroused and hoped Master did not notice as she quickly slipped a finger twixt her petals.

Pet, too, grew more aroused at the sight; she was now quite agitated—how she ached for a soothing tongue, or to be penetrated—anything to ease the unbearable throbbing twixt her legs.

"Slave, your playmate is eager to join you—why don't you invite her in?"

And with that, slave beckoned, "Come here, Pet! Come and play with me!" Pet tore off her clothes… "Ah—no, Pet," interrupted her Master, "Leave on your dungarees."

What!? Pet's heart sank—how desperate she was to soothe the pounding ache in her groin—leave her pants on!? Has Master gone daft!? But no! Pet immediate fought to dash such a prospect from her silly mind: Master's cruelty has never been without reason—albeit the reason could, at times, be for himself, alone. She recalled his severe punishment earlier in the day—how harsh it seemed, and yet how utterly pleasurable it was. This confusion of her senses made Pet's heart quicken and her vulva swell. Re-buttoning the top of her jeans, she flung herself at her water nymph slave, momentarily carrying them both under the surface; they bounced back up, grabbing and wrestling with one another, like river otters splashing and squealing and laughing.

Now and then they'd glance over at Master; he appeared to be rooting around in his satchel, looking for something; or he would just stand there, hand pulling his chin, staring intently and his girls. Clearly up to something, he…

Slave and Pet's rambunctiousness turned to more sensual play: Pet floated slave in her arms, and nibbled at her nipples through her soaked T-shirt while running her fingers through slave's hair, which looked like sea grass waving side to side. The sound of the waterfall made Pet restless; she went to touch herself, foiled by the heavy, wet jeans. Oh! Why is Master denying her pleasure!? Pet was determined to get off—what if she were to do so, vicariously, through slave…? Pet glided her hand down slave's belly, twixt slave's labia, and gently rubbed her clit. With a moan, slave twisted and rolled Pet in the water, took Pet's breasts in her hands and squeezed and massaged them, pressing and pulling; she took one into her mouth and suckled. Pet plunged her fingers into slave's pussy, causing slave to bite Pet's nipple—oh, how soothing such pain can be! Pet pulled her fingers out and sucked off the sweet water and musk, wishing she could finger herself and taste her own juices—damn these cursed, soaked jeans!!

"Slave! Bring Pet here." Master's voice—but where was he?

Slave swam around behind Pet, took her by her shoulders, and guided her to the waterfall. Through the transparent curtain of water, Master reached his arm out and hoisted Pet up to the natural rock platform on which he stood. There, Pet discovered Master's plan: a rigging of rope net and cuffs against the cliff—not unlike a giant spider's web, and Pet was his prey…

Part IV

Master had disrobed; his nakedness was stunning: skin glistening with waterfall mist, his member standing erect. Pet could not help but stare, until she realized this might upset her sister-slave, and so she held her eyes downcast. Oh how Pet desired, as surely as did slave, to stroke and kiss Master's great root.

The cold made Pet shiver: the breeze created by the rushing water and low, late-afternoon sun teased her hardened nipples; her drenched jeans felt so terribly uncomfortable. Pet tried to cover her pale bosom with her hands to warm them, but Master would have none of that. "Pet, No!" he snapped. Pet immediately brought her hands down to her sides, upon whence Master's stern look warmed. Slave licked her lips with anticipation—clearly they were enjoying how the cold air made Pet's breasts look so round and perky. It occurred to Pet that her attempt at comfort had momentarily denied her owners their pleasure; now she worried Master would punish her for this thoughtlessness.

She needn't worry long: Master roughly grabbed Pet's wrists and deftly secured her to his web, facing outward toward the waterfall.

"Slave, please remove Pet's jeans." An evil smile spread across slave's face as she struggled to remove Pet's jeans, which had tightened against her skin and were putting up a fight. Slave pulled down enough to expose the puff of hair twixt Pet's legs; she paused, gazing hungrily at the delta; she looked up at Master, questioningly. "Yes, my girl, but quickly now—we still have work to do, and the sun is going down." Slave caressed Pet's mound; with her thumb she pulled back Pet's clit hood to expose her pearl. She exhaled warm breath upon the treasure and then kissed it with long, slow licks. Pet grew aroused by the pleasant shock of heat against her cold skin, and slave gladly lapped up the honey that seeped from within.

Stroking his tumescent cock, Master reached for the set of nipple tweezers dangling from the net; he flickered his tongue against Pet's nipples to make them stand out even further, then applied each tweezer's clamp, pushing the rings completely tight to hold the tines in place; Pet cried out in pain; slave pulled herself away in surprise. "Tut, tut, little Pet!" admonished Master, "It's not as if I were applying those monstrously cruel Japanese clover clamps!" (Master smiled wryly—unbeknownst to Pet, he had plans for those, later…)

Pet protested, "Please, Sir, I beg you!" Master was a strong disciplinarian, indeed, but not a sadist—not to mention his having to stifle a giggle at the pathetic look of his dear Pet's pleading eyes—so he pulled each ring down ever so slightly; Pet winced at the sting of blood rushing back into her abused nipples. Just as she regained her composure, Master yanked on the chain; Pet wailed in pain—and then smiled. "There, there, little Pet," cooed Master as he cupped a hand in the waterfall and directed its cool stream to soothe Pet's flaming nipples, "I am simply ensuring they hold." Master then clipped a leash to the chain and handed the end to slave. A twinkle grew in slave's eye as she hooked her index finger through the loop… Pet's heart raced…

Tug, tug—Pet released a guttural howl at the intense pleasure-pain.

Master kneeled down to kiss slave, and instructed her to complete her task. Slave roughly yanked the jeans down to Pet's ankles—no easy task, being they were now so very tight. Pet's waterlogged, pale skin appeared extra white, and the pants down around her ankles made her feel far more exposed than were she completely naked.

Master then pulled another tweezer from the niche—this one a single, forked prong with a little bell on the end. He parted Pet's labia, but found her vulva was now far too slippery with nectar; Master knelt down—Pet felt a rush of heat at the sight of Master prostrate before her!—and proceeded to thoroughly clean Pet with his tongue. He worked very carefully at removing the viscous honey—Pet tried to will herself to secrete more, to keep him going. But alas, Master stood up and twixt thumb and forefinger pinched her clit-hood tight, again revealing the pink pearl beneath, to which he directly applied the tweezer. Pet yelped at the nipping metal; the little bell ting-tinged as she futilely thrashed about. Master stepped back, and stroked the hair of his beloved slave huddled against his leg, as they both took in the vision of their prey trapped and squirming in his web.

"S-Sir, may I please speak?" Pet shyly asked; Master raised his eyebrow in assent. "This sudden cold against my skin, it gives me cause to… to…" Embarrassment overtook her. "Yes, Pet—speak." "Sir, may I please again relieve myself?"

Master's eyes twinkled: "Slave! Down!" Master commanded, as if to a dog; without a moment's hesitation, slave fully kowtowed before Pet.

Pet blushed as confusion gave way to recognition of what she was to do. The cold, combined with her shyness, and added to that, the pain of the clit tweezer, initially prevented her from performing; but then, at once came streaming out a shower of liquid gold that splashed upon slave's back and trickled down her shoulders. Slave cooed at the penetrating warmth, and looked up in reverence at her impounded (and yet, dominating?) Pet. She allowed the last of Pet's yellow water christen her breasts, and then arched backward through the waterfall and into the pool, tugging on the leash as she fell. Pet cried out in painful delight as the nipple tweezers tore away.

Master released Pet from the cuffs, and lowered her back into the pool, holding her afloat by the shoulders. Slave ducked under the waterfall and then popped up between Pet's legs, which were still bound by the jeans around her ankles, and spread Pet's knees open wide. Together, they positioned Pet so that her pelvis was directly under the waterfall. The pressure felt like a hundred tongues—nature's vibrator!—and set the little clit bell tinkling. Slave firmly locked her arms around Pet's legs, with the jeans acting as restraints, to keep Pet's pussy in position; a task that grew most challenging, for slave, as Pet squirmed a great deal upon Master's inserting a glass dildo deep into her tight little rosebud of an anus. (How wonderful, to be so violated!)

Master gripped the hair on Pet's mound and pulled back to further expose her clit to the waterfall; Pet linked her arms around Master's neck to hold herself up as he kissed her deeply whilst his other hand played the dildo in and out of her ass. The pounding water, the pounding hearts, the swirling and probing of tongues and rods, the biting clit tweezer—it all became too much for Pet and she screamed from deep within the core of her body into her Master's kiss, arching her hips, digging her nails into Master's neck, thrashing her jeans-bound legs about; a great, violent shudder as her body was wracked with the electric jolts of lingering orgasm.

Slave freed Pet's ankles from the confines of the jeans and removed the appliances; then, together with her Master, held the gasping, exhausted body of their now-spent, beloved Pet; secondary spasms flashed through Pet's body as she sobbed, so completely and profoundly overwhelmed by pleasure and love.

After what felt, to her, like hours—even days—and with the sun now far behind the treeline, Pet regained her strength, enough that the three of them could step out of the pool and gather up their gear. Master pulled three dry terry robes from his satchel; they wrapped themselves in comforting warmth, and tiredly, gingerly made their way back to the cabin. Pet lit the stove and served up steaming mugs of hot cocoa spiked with cognac. All three hearts and bodies soothed, they snuggled up in bed and allowed themselves to be carried off to sleep.

...

That is, until Pet was awakened by the delicious, squishy sound of Master's cock plunging his slave's ever-ready pussy. Pet kissed slave tenderly to hush her moans, and cooed lovingly as she watched Master's body shudder and his face contort in powerful climax.

Lying back on her pillow, Pet fingered her moistened, slightly sore vulva and pondered this witnessing of such a touching, intimate little moment—it may very well have been the most satisfying of the day.

She drifted to sleep, fantasizing about what lied ahead, tomorrow.

THE TURNING OF DESMOND

By Akasha Vampyrssa

An excerpt from Second Pulse

Jake grabbed my arms and pinned them to the door. His body pressed tight behind me.

"Don't turn around, Desmond. Please, just stop." His breathy pleas whispered in my ear.

I could feel him harden behind me. My brain raced to process what was happening. His breath was hot on my neck. His hands were bruising my wrists.

"Desmond…I need you to… Please, just... I need you… Just be calm." His voice quivered with forced control.

Be calm? I had this half-crazed asshole pinning me to the door. How was I supposed to be calm?

"Fuck the ceremony, you are mine!" Those words scaled down my spine like nails cutting flesh. He easily overpowered me, dragging me across the room. I tried to protest but it was no good. He threw me so hard on the bed; I thought it was going to break under the force. Before I could protest, Jake was on top of me, holding me down.

"Desy, you have no idea what you have awakened in me. And for this, I am almost sorry. Almost."

Jake snatched my arm and suckled the blood-stained fingertips. Intense pulses shot straight to my groin, awakening me. I found myself growing with excitement. My fear only increased the pleasure. Jake smiled as he felt me respond. His smile was dark and held so much warning, yet I was not listening. I couldn't give a shit about anything at that point. As long as he was going to pleasure me, I didn't care what he did.

Jake ripped off my pants. I didn't fight him. I wanted him so much. The desire burning, threatening me to end so early. Please! For the love of the Gods, please don't let this end! The thought drifted through my mind. I never wanted this moment to stop. I felt so full of ecstasy; so full of need. In that moment, I didn't care what he did to me as long as he never stopped touching me.

As he rolled me over, my excitement brushed against the bed. I felt the urge to keep rubbing and thrusting but Jake stopped me.

"Not yet, Desy." He whispered in my ear as his body pressed against mine. His lips, soft and gentle, kissed my back. He let his lips trace my spine sending throbbing waves through my skin. He sank down and spread me, his tongue flicking over the sensitive skin. His fingers were learning my body, stroking my desire. His soft kisses became little bites here and there. My back arched, lifting my hips in desperation. I wasn't sure I could handle much more before I exploded.

I felt him enter me; my moans betrayed me. I grasped the bedding beneath me, sweat building on my forehead. "Take me! All of me," I yelled. I had become another person. Like a primal version of who I once was. I didn't know who this person was under Jake. My hips moved in rhythm. His thrusting became relentless. The deeper he went, the harder I pushed against him. He grabbed my hips and drilled deep inside me. I couldn't take it anymore. My body threatened to give out if I did not release this pleasure. I cried out begging him to take all of me.

Jake obeyed. His entire body on mine, thrusting harder and deeper than allowed. His teeth sank deep in my neck causing my seed to spill on the bed, guttural moans vibrating my chest. The burning in my neck took over in hot waves of ecstasy. The room began to spin. With one final thrust, he filled me until he had nothing left to give. I was spent. My body, trying to fight him as he held on, had no energy left. I could not move. His strength holding me in place while he sucked at my neck, stealing my life force. The sounds were swimming. I kept trying to pull myself away but it was no use. My arms were shaking. I couldn't move. Jake, still deep inside me, only held tighter.

My eyes began closing. I had no control. I could hear Jake in the far distance, like he had gone down the hall and was yelling at me in a Mason jar.

"Desmond…Drink!"

THE CHASTENING OF JADE WOODS

By Max Silver

Jade Woods peered past the curtains, just enough for them to see the audience without the audience seeing them. Shadows bearing flashy grins and fistfuls of dollar bills smirked through the sultry haze of smoke and devilish laughter.

Normally Jade would not be concerned by a rambunctious throng of spoiled perverts, but something made them reluctant to leave the safety of the curtains tonight… A jittery sensation tingled through their arms and down to the warm, soft, squishy spot between their bare and quivering thighs.

It was a silly outfit, Jade thought to themself, as they wobbled atop translucent high-heels, wearing diaphanous pink lace to go with their heliotrope hair and the tight-fitting black corset around their doughy waist. They would have preferred to wear something more androgynous tonight, as they felt comfortable with clothing that came without generic-gender labels attached. This was one of the reasons Jade preferred stripping for a living. As they removed each layer, they felt less confined to the bindings of a dominant civilization both predominantly binary and terribly boring.

Perhaps it would have been easier to wear slacks, rather than a flimsy skirt that barely covered the pot leaf on their callipygian left lower mound. Jade had performed burlesque at open venues all over the country, and it wasn't the venue that was racking their nerves… it was a small, humming device, wedged deep between the crevasse between their sticky legs.

Of course, Jade could have removed the electric plug at any point in time, but Jade knew that Master was waiting at the front of the audience, and they would rather face embarrassment than to fail their Master's test… Who knew what diabolical scheme he would hatch next for their punishment? No, Jade would not capitulate this time. Not after the last. Jade Woods was a professional, and they would perform their burlesque act no matter how intense the vibrations resonating from the device tucked deep inside their juicy cunt.

"Howdy folx!" Jade nervously greeted the audience. Those sinners in the crowd who had attended a bawdy show before hollered like sluts and demons liberated in hell. Meanwhile, those bourgeoisie in the audience who had never witnessed burlesque; a night of grotesque parody, freakish variety, mock-verses of a society otherwise portrayed to them as normal in their mundane lives, became so enthralled by this slattern affair they had no choice but to yank out their wallets and arm themselves with fistfuls of cash in eager anticipation of the evening's debauchery to come.

"Oops!" Jade awkwardly straddled the microphone to keep it from wiggling too much, causing their wholesome derriere to jiggle stage left. Jade swore in their head at the Master for making them wear this atrocious outfit. It did nothing to conceal Jade's sumptuous ass. At the same time Jade Woods loved it, lifting their pink skirt to the stage-lights and mooning everyone, showing off that cherry-red thong drenched between their rotund cheeks, pressed tightly to the outer lips of Jade's tender, piquant vale.

Oh, no! Jade recalled, *I better not let them notice that there's a wire trailing out from the device in my wet pussy. On second thought, if anyone asks, I'll just insist it's a bloody tampon string. I'm sure they'll believe me. I'll keep it snug in there until Master comes to pull it out with his teeth.* Suddenly, Jade felt a zap under their panties. To their shock, this caused them to bend over and inadvertently moan into the microphone.

"Oooohhh…" The audience moaned back with lecherous glee.

"Fuck!" Jade cursed the Master under their breath. *That asshole! What did they do to deserve this sort of humiliation?* Carefully, Jade Woods unhooked the microphone from the stand.

"Welcome to the show!" Jade's eyelid twitched as the Master pressed the button again. Jade Woods sprang into the air, causing their petite tits to jostle atop the tight fitting black corset. Jade had taped black X's over their nipples. As the technology pulsed within their tingling vulva, they felt the need to massage their breasts in order to prevent their hard nipples from rubbing against the adhesive. Their heart was palpitating. They hadn't even performed the first step of their act yet, and already Jade Woods felt they might pee, if not squirt, on stage!

"S-s-s-stop…"Jade mumbled, before uncontrollably emitting another high pitched moan to a roar of applause. The Master was deliberately punishing them. Jade could see the button in the palm of his hand. Another click, and Jade screamed so loud they had to deep throat the microphone in order to stop their titillating vocals from getting the audience too excited.

Many were cheering, however some were exchanging queer glances at one another, arching eyebrows and wondering if Jade Woods was okay. Did they become possessed by awkward stage fright, or was there a lustful temptation deep down under that was causing the MC to grope their pussy in plain sight while sloppily gagging on that dirty, dirty microphone?

At last, another electric tremor caused a light trail of urine to run down the length of their sweaty inner thigh, and Jade Woods could not stand it anymore. They drove their fingers deep into their cooter, grasping with all five appendages for the insatiable instrument of torture. The audience applauded with nervous, if not salacious laughter. One of the derelicts shouted, "Whatcha got in your purse, Jade Woods? Can you probe a bit deeper?"

Other performers behind the counter murmured in shock. Why the hell was Jade Woods fisting themself in public? At last, Jade had a firm grip on the alien object, and after plummeting wrist-deep into their moist ravine Jade Woods yanked the electric toy out from their seeping pussy and squirted all over the floor. Drenched in their own sea of cum, Jade Woods sank to their knees, and despite the humiliation of being put on display in such an unexpected fashion, the burlesquer was relieved that the apparatus had finally exited their dripping orifice.

Jade's relief did not last for long, as they heard a slow, uncanny clap in an otherwise stunned and silent audience.

"Well done," the Master rose from his seat, and others wearing lacy masks with bunny ears and devilish horns joined in on congratulating Jade by clapping their hands in a slow, nonchalant rhythm. "You have passed the Master's test."

"I have?" Jade asked with astonishment, "but I...you said...before the show I had to wear it inside my pussy for the entire act."

The Master scratched his Satanic beard and smiled with a flash of fangs. "I knew you would not be able to withstand the power of the Electrofuck 6900, as I had set it to its highest level. You failed to hold it in, but you lasted as long as possible, and in doing your best you passed the test by failing it."

"Why did you turn it up so high, you fuckin dick," Jade Woods felt dizzy and disoriented from cumming so hard.

The Master nodded. "Silence, you disobedient glitter-whore. Finish your performance. Do you want the show to go on or not?" And he walked right up on the center stage and stood over Jade Woods, his shadow protruding over their bare shoulders and the bodacious curves of their ripe bottom.

"Y-yes," Jade answered, much to the joyful and lascivious praise of the leering throng.

Without further ado, Jade's Master unzipped his trousers and unsheathed his cock, slapping Jade across the cheek with the meat of his bulging shaft before plunging the entire thing deep down Jade's gaping throat amidst the cheering, taunting, and uproar of a frenzied crowd.

Jade Woods gagged as their lips wrapped around the length of Master's cock. They coughed up some spittle as the Master grabbed their pinkish hair and began thrusting and thrusting, brutally shoving their face deep into his hairy sack. At one point, he drew away from their salivating lips, for all behind the curtain to witness the streams of saliva cascading from their panting throat, make-up and rouge an awful mess on their spit and cum-covered visage.

The other burlesquers scoffed at the effrontery, as the Master reached around with a black latex glove, and inserted two lubricated fingers deep into Jade's holes… one in their soaked pussy, the other in their tight butthole. Jade Woods wanted to scream with embarrassment, but before they knew it the Master had stuffed his balls in their mouth, and Jade felt compelled to start sucking his salty testicles, lathering their tongue in circles and reaching out to taste the taint before greedily licking the rim of Master's asshole.

"Tell them," the Master commanded, "tell the audience how much of a filthy whore you are."

"I'm a filthy whore!" Jade Woods cried out, "Please fuck me Master, please fuck me with your cock in the middle of the stage in front of everyone!"

"Not yet," the Master chided them, "first, you must be devoured!"

The Master wrapped his fingers around Jade Woods and roughly lifted them to their wobbling knees. Before they could cry out, they were flung towards the audience, like a piece of meat to a school of sharks, who began feeding and feasting hungrily on Jade's supple flesh, reaching out with money-grubbing hands to squeeze Jade's petite breasts, stick fingers in Jade's whorish mouth, squeeze Jade's ass and slap Jade's sweltering pussy to their liking.

Part of Jade wanted to cry out, but another part of Jade Woods craved for more. Jade felt like such an avaricious slut. They wanted to be touched like this, to be ravaged by the audience. As Jade thought these dirty things, they became presently aware that Master had dragged them back to the center stage. Jade got down to their knees, assuming the position for fellatio, but to their surprise he whipped them around.

Jade was now facing the audience. In a flash they felt the Master's tongue licking their clitoris! Jade moaned loudly, biting their lip as the Master inserted three lubricated fingers into their exposed cunt, fingering their G spot as he continued lapping their labia with a slippery tongue.

Jade quivered and moaned with orgasm as the Master slipped his tongue inside their hood, flicking the clit until they could hardly stand it and came in the Master's face. At last, as Jade was on the verge of yet another pulsing orgasm, the Master stood and inserted his stone-hard dick into Jade's gaping pussy. He grabbed onto the sides of their jiggling ass and began pumping and pumping Jade so they cried out and squealed uncontrollably. "Yes, Master, please, fuck me harder!"

Presently, several audience members wearing bunny masks and devil horns walked onto the stage. Jade opened their mouth to ask why they felt like this was an opportune moment to climb on stage and interrupt the performance, when one of the audience members took out his aged, shriveled penis and shoved it along with entire scrotum into Jade's mouth.

The audience members took turns having Jade suck them off. Meanwhile Master restrained Jade Woods with both arms roughly behind their back. Jade could do nothing to prevent the audience from holding their head whilst groping their tits and throatfucking them.

All the while the Master kept forcing his cock deeper inside Jade's wet, succulent pussy, until Jade felt the need to piss. Almost as if reading their thoughts, the Master pulled his cock out from Jade's pulsating cunt, making them squirt all over the stage.

"Lick it," the Master instructed them, and Jade Woods crawled over to the pool of their own tangy fluids and began to lap up their cum and piss like a dog. Meanwhile, one of the masked audience members, who it was Jade had no idea, came over and shoved his cock into Jade's loose and slippery cunt.

A whole train of them, stuffing their cock and balls into Jade's slutty holes, filling Jade's mouth and pussy at the same time and fingering Jade's dirty asshole. Jade found themself in a delirium of spurting orgasms and embarrassing queefs. They were not sure how much time passed, but soon they were lying on the stage on their back. Master was pounding them on top in missionary position with Jade's clear plastic heels high over his head. Jade's eyes rolled to the back of their head. They could not stop moaning with pleasure, overcome with the impulse to be fucked and used like a ragdoll.

As he kept fucking Jade hard, the gang of participants all took turns shouting profanities at them. "Dirty slut! You probably adore having so much attention on your fat ass and your luscious lips."

"Yeah, give it to them good, and you, devour that cum you voracious whore!" Then one of them came up to Jade Woods and dipped his balls into their mouth. As he did, a luke-warm trickle of jizz spurted from the tip of his cock and landed right on Jade Wood's forehead.

"What the fuck?" Jade muttered. Master's cock was still throbbing deep inside them, keeping their pussy warm and juicy as he kept forcing it deeper and deeper into their saturated lair.

Jade Woods felt compelled to play the part of a late-night cum-dumpster so they sucked the stranger's balls dry until he had finished cumming on their soggy face and hot pink hair. When the scoundrel lifted his scrotum, Jade opened their mouth as another cock was forced into their gagging throat. It came so quickly Jade had to spit the jizz swiftly out from their blurry lips before it funneled through their nostrils.

Another cock slapped Jade in the eye, and a bloated penis released a geyser of ecstasy fluids which rained over Jade as another fired adjacent to their ear and a fourth completely missed and came on seated members of the audience.

By the end of it, Jade's face was plastered with spunk, and the Master had lifted them into doggy style once again. Three more audience members with dicks thrust themselves into Jade's mouth and came on their face and their sloping back. An audience member with a pussy rubbed her filthy cunt in Jade's mouth and pissed all over them. Finally, Master grunted and released his seed in Jade's quivering pussy, and as Jade gasped, trembled, and moaned for more the audience stood in applause.

"Thank you, thank you," the Master took a swift bow, and then lifted a sticky Jade Woods to their wobbling feet. "Now...we'll have a brief intermission.

Jade Woods spoke with pearls of jizz running down their nude physique and onto the messy stage, "could someone please hand me a fucking towel?"

GETTING HAMMERED

By Ev Joy Lokadottr

The air was redolent with the scent of freshly-cut wood.

The sound of a grinder whirred sporadically in the distance.

Putting her paintbrush down, the young woman wiped at the sweat beading her brow, and cursed as she felt the all-too familiar sensation of wet paint smearing on her skin. Again.

"Oh joy, another facial," she started to grumble irritably, but a giggle seeped out of the edges of her voice.

"And I wasn't invited?" a quiet voice, smooth and sensual, poured over her. She shivered as if it had caressed her skin. She was so hyper vigilant normally, how did he always sneak up behind her? He moved so quietly. So controlled.

"Um. I mean. I thought you were busy?" she stammered lamely.

Yeah, really smooth, she told herself. She was an accomplished writer, at least in the blogosphere, and pretty good at holding forth at parties. Why did this man seem to rob her of all her erudite wit? Oh, she knew. She knew very well. He'd gotten under her skin. She wanted him. She wanted him to take her, she knew he was a dom and she felt the call to open herself to him, expose her soft, white underbelly. It scared her because she wanted it. It scared her because she didn't know if she could stop, once she said "yes." The fear itself was a heady intoxicant.

She trembled briefly, before forcing herself to be still.

"Well, I am working. We are at work. Slut." The last was so quiet; she couldn't quite convince herself he'd really said it.

"Wait, did you... uh. I'm working, see? I painted this whole window frame." She showed off her work, which she took a great deal of pride in. Careful, steady, smooth strokes had coated the frame in a lovely matte white.

Matte.

"Fuck," he said "that's matte. It's supposed to be glossy."

Her heart dropped into her feet. She'd messed up. She was sure she'd picked the right bucket of paint! Was he going to fire her? Send her away? "I'm sorry, I'm so, so sorry, I, I'll fix it, please, let me just fix it, I should have paid more attention, I didn't realize, I'm sorry!"

"It's all right. You didn't know. Accidents happen. Calm down... Breathe. Good girl."

The tension around her eyes eased, and the cringing expression on her face began to fade away.

"But... I'm sorry. Can I fix it?"

"Yes, you want the bucket with the strip of tape on it that says trim. The green tape, not the blue. Be a good girl now." He pulled a rag out of his pocket and wiped her forehead. As though her face was his to clean. Caretaker. The tension in her shoulders eased. He wasn't too angry with her. Maybe it would be ok.

"There you go," he smoothed her hair away from her eyes, "now, back to work." She took a shaky breath, pulling herself together. He hadn't yelled. He hadn't slapped her so hard her ears rang and her neck hurt and told her she was lazy and making excuses. He hadn't threatened to send her away, and never speak to her again. He hadn't told her all about how she fell short, wasn't good enough, and wasn't thinking. Hadn't complained about how much of a pain she was, how difficult she made his life. Hadn't told her she was a disappointment.

Why she was thinking these things, she didn't know. She shouldn't. This was her boss. She shook her head. Why did she think he might act like that?

"I've been doing this decades before you were even alive," the words of her own dom rang out in her head. "You won't ever meet someone like me again. I know what you're thinking, I know what you are and what you're feeling, and I know it better than you do. So stop giving me bullshit. And stop crying. I hate wimpy, whining subs. You're not allowed to cry. If you don't stop right now, you will leave, and I won't talk to you for a month."

Abandoned. He would abandon her. He would take himself away from her. And part of her would be relieved. How about that?

But also devastated. She'd opened herself to him. And he'd made her feel things she had never felt before. But he'd also torn her to pieces, again and again. She never knew what words might set him off. She never knew how to tell him something scared her or upset her without him shredding her, leaving her with panic attacks, scrambling, begging for forgiveness, doing things that made her feel so awful inside, just to try to make him proud and happy again, just to please him.

He never stayed pleased for long.

Focus, she told herself, *focus*.

Steadily, she applied paint to wood.

And now, though she'd grown so strong, it was a brittle strength. She felt like a sword that was heated too hot and cooled too fast. Run through the crucible and the forge again and again, but ready to snap if anything hard slammed against her. And so she was there, terrified her boss was going to fire her because she painted a window frame the wrong color.

But it was more than that, too. It was more than the impossibly high standards she always held herself to. It was more than how hard she pushed herself, since that relentless will, that driving angry force with no compassion for herself that kept her alive for so many years. It was also the fact that, she had to admit to herself, she really did want to please him. More than an employee wants to please an employer. Something in his energy drew her to him. She wanted to serve well, and to know she had done well. She wanted to feel his breath in her ear, his hands sliding over her flesh, his cock pushing into her-

Focus.

She breathed in deep, and let go of her mind, as much as she could. It wasn't like the times when she could submit, and only experience, only feel and do as she was told. But still, it was peace. Mind, no mind. Let all the intrusive thoughts pass her by. Up and down, the little brush strokes went. A long, smooth stroke to sweep up the inevitable paint drips that marred her work. Up, and down. Color over color.

Time passed.

She was close to done when thoughts intruded that she decided to let in. Her heart, skipping in her chest. Her eyes, dilating ever so slightly. Her pulse, hammering in her throat. Just a few little words. "You'd better leave now, before I put my hand on your throat, slut." She fled, because she wanted it so badly. She knew if she stayed, her knees would turn to jelly and her brain would turn to mush. She'd drown in a flood of endorphins and he could do whatever he wanted.

All of the things she wanted too. Just too tempting. She'd had to run. But now, with him just in the next room, her boldness returned, since she wasn't looking at him, wasn't talking to him.

She whipped out her phone, pulled a creamy, massive breast out of her shirt, and snapped a photo.

An impish smile spread across her face as she hit the "send" button.

A ding.

The grinder stopped.

A sigh.

The grinder started again.

Too much? Maybe it was too much. She'd sent them before, but... she'd messed up today. She didn't want to push, didn't want to get on his nerves. She was always being accused of topping from the bottom. Always being told she wasn't a real submissive because she had desires of her own. She felt her jaw clench, and the all-too-familiar tension headache started to pulse at her temples.

Well, maybe she was a rotten submissive, because she wanted a lot. She wanted to feel safe; she wanted to be fucked, long and hard and mercilessly, over and over again by man after man as other men held her down. She wanted consistency. She wanted to stop thinking for a while. She wanted to cum. She wanted to be bound.

She wanted to be held as red welts and tooth marks faded on her skin. She wanted her body to be seen as acceptable. No, *hot.* Scars and sagging skin and all, because that was what she lived in. She wanted to be heard. She wanted to be a good girl.

She wanted to know she could let go without falling into a trap. She wanted to speak her feelings and needs without it blowing up in her face. She wanted to obey. She wanted to be pinned to the wall and violated. She wanted strong hands on her body, using her, taking her, possessing her.

She wanted to be told it was all right if she cried, to let it out, to share her feelings, and to work through them, instead of being attacked for it. She wanted to not cry so goddamn much. She wanted to wrap her lips around a lovely cock and suck and lick and stroke until the man she was sucking was twitching and shuddering with the need to cum, his balls high and tight and full, his voice telling her to suck like a good girl, *yes, yes, yes,* take it all.

She'd painted the final corner of the frame three times, and the brush was in her hand, paint dribbling down her wrist.

"I'd say it's done," he said behind her. Shivers ran down her spine. How did he *do* that?

"I-I yes sorry, done! It's glossy now. Better, right? I'm so sorry I painted it the wrong color, really, *really* I am."

"You know, we have a bit of a problem here. I told you it was ok. And yet, you didn't believe me." He was behind her, pressed up against her, his hand sliding around her body, holding her in place. His breath in her ear.

"I think maybe you want to be punished, to make it all better. You need to learn to breathe and let go and trust me when I tell you something's ok."

She relaxed a little bit. It really was ok.

"You're still going to be punished, though."

"What, I am? I... why sir? What-what uh... what will you do?" her voice was soft, weak, she hoped she wasn't whining. Her heart was in her throat.

"It seems my minion has been sending dirty photos at work."

"Oh, I'm sorry, if you don't like that, I'll stop, I shouldn't have, I'm sorry, I promise I was working hard."

"I know you were. And no, I *did* like the photo. Very much. That's the problem, you see, you left me with this." He pressed up against her, and oh yes, *that.* His cock was making its presence known quite effectively, pressed up against the small of her back. She felt him slide down her body, just a tiny bit.

"There are consequences for sluts that tease. I'm not going to punish you about the fucking window. I intend to make you forget all about that, little cockwhore. That's what you are. A fuckslut. And you teased me. You made me hard. Get up. Now. Follow me."

Not waiting for her to reply, he let go and moved away. The heat of him was replaced with a chill that spread across her back and had nothing to do with the ambient temperature of the room.

Rising on legs that suddenly seemed so very unsteady, she swallowed hard, and turned. He was staring at her, arms crossed over his chest, eyes burning into her, and suddenly she felt so exposed. She licked her lips.

"Mhm," he murmured softly, perhaps to himself. Like he'd seen exactly what he expected to see. He turned and sauntered away, to the unfinished basement room with its tall, wide, concrete ledge, almost big enough to be a small stage. She followed him and paused in the doorway, nervously glancing up the stairs. He reached out and wrapped his hand around her throat, then fisted her hair with his other hand.

Pulling her close to him, so close, he murmured in her ear, "There's no one here today but us. You're all alone, with me. Breathe. You will do as I say, like a good slut, won't you? Come here. That's a good girl." There she was, shaky-breathed but coaxed closer, closer, her eyes beginning to glaze over, she felt herself slipping, sliding down into that place. That place where she wasn't her own any more. That place where she was free.

His hand glided over her body, up, and down, fingers trailing across the breasts she had so impertinently teased him with. Slowly they traced the contours of her waist, her hips. They turned, and the legs of her shorts and panties were bunched in his fists. With a sudden, sharp yank, he pulled them down around her ankles.

She yelped, and started to cover herself, but he said "Sssh. Shhhhhh. No, no, be a good girl, here," and pulled her hands behind her back. "That's a good slut. Good girl, now open your legs wide for me. Show me that sweet little pussy you have sent me so many pictures of."

"Yes sir," she breathed, and opened her legs more, her face flushed. Why did she get so shy? Scared of rejection, maybe, and filled with excitement about what could happen.

He ran his fingers up her thighs, taking his time, savoring her. Breathing her in. Slipping a finger between the folds of her sweet little cunt, he exposed her wetness. Often her body didn't produce enough, even when she was turned on, but at that moment, she was hot and slick.

"Mmm, you're wet. Very nice, slut." One hand still lightly toying with her between her legs, he planted his other on the small of her back, and pulled them both backwards until he was against the ledge. From there, he let go a moment.

"Stay." he said, and sat on the ledge, his feet resting on a platform so that his legs took the shape of the seat of a chair.

He patted his lap. "Bend over and lie down here."

"Are... you sure this is a good idea? What if someone... um." her words trailed off. She shook. Her pussy glistened. She wanted to run. She wanted to be taken.

His eyes narrowed as he took in her hesitation. "Breathe. It's all right. Come here. You want to be good and take your punishment, don't you, little slut?"

"Yes... yes sir."

He wrapped his arm around her butt, grasping her hip, and slid his other hand up between her legs, parting her lips, snaking two fingers up to her tight, wet entrance. She gasped, and he pressed his fingers into her, inexorably entering her, violating her, impaling her. He hooked his fingers forward. She was caught. With his other arm he pulled her down to his lap, and there she went. She had no choice.

Ass in the air, beet red, her breathing was fast, shuddering. "Your job right now is to take what I give you, and be taken, cockwhore," he told her. "Feel it, take it like a good girl. There. That's right."

She felt her breathing slow a little and began to relax, going limp over his thighs. Letting go, as she craved to, sinking down into- **smack** the first stinging slap made her white, full cheeks jiggle, and she yelped softly. He murmured a sound of approval when her pussy clenched over the fingers holding her in place.

"You're an eager cockhungry slut, aren't you?" his hand rose and fell, spanking her ass. She wiggled, and he chuckled, moving his fingers inside of her.

"You have to ask if you want to cum, do you understand me? Don't you dare cum unless you have permission, slut. Beg for it. Understand?"

"Yes sir, yes," she breathed. She was nowhere near close though she was so turned on. Her dom almost never gave her an orgasm. The few times he did give her a chance, the pain would often overwhelm it, or she would get close, but not make it in time, and he would tell her it was her problem, not his, that she failed to cum. The times she had, it had been epic, but it was rare. She hoped she'd be allowed to this time, with this man.

As the blows fell, she began to pant. Her butt was so warm and red. His skillful fingers seemed to know just where to go to tease and drive her higher.

"Please," she whimpered, "Please... please more." She tore the words from herself, adrenaline and endorphins both surging, her heart wanting to pound its way free of her chest.

"How many more spanks do you want? Tell me."

Her mind didn't want to work. "Three, sir?"

"Mmm." Three heavy swats to her wiggling ass, and the fingers came out of her pussy. She whimpered in protest, and could feel him smirking, somehow. She started to rise when the hand that had been inside, now on the middle of her back, her pushed down.

Three fingers plunged into her cunt, deep and hard. Once, twice, three times, and then she was empty again.

"Please, please!"

"How many?" he asked.

"Seven! Please, seven!"

And so he swatted her ass, each strike was harder to take than the next, and she shook, little cries escaping her lips as she gritted her teeth.

Seven hard thrusts into her pussy. Her eyes rolled back into her head.

"That's a good girl, that's a very good girl, taking it for me. You can take it for me can't you? You will. And I will take you. You know that I will. It's inevitable. You're already mine to devour, slut. How many do you want to take for me?"

"Ten, please, ten!"

She was crying out with each strike, and then breathing, hard and fast through her nose, digging her fingers into his calf muscle as she braced herself. She would take this. She would take it all for him. For *him.*

And then the fingers again, savage, deep, relentless, her pussy spasming around them, she was closer, closer, *closer...*

"Good girl, you took it all. Up. Sit up in my lap, turn around. Put your arm around my shoulders and hold on. I want to see your face. I want to watch you cum, fuckmeat."

She turned and sat in his lap. She was afraid she might hurt him, but her weight didn't seem to be a problem for him. He didn't give her time to think about it. One arm wrapped behind her back and around her side, giving him access to her breasts.

He rolled her breast in his hand and then reached down the front of her shirt. "I want these pulled out of your shirt," he instructed. She pulled them out with her free hand, struggling with the task, but she managed. Looking up at him, he saw approval in his eyes.

Approval and hunger. Lust. Intense focus. It was hard to stare into his eyes. They looked too deep into her. But she wanted him there. She forced herself to look. He wanted to see into her eyes. She wanted to give him that. She didn't know if he would really make her cum, but the need was building inside of her, fading a little now, but not enough. Not enough to stop her from squirming on his lap, and feeling his very, very hard cock. She froze.

He chuckled, realizing just what she'd noticed.

"You want it, don't you, slut?" he whispered in her ear. She shivered and moaned, and when he looked back into her eyes, she breathed a "yes."

He ran his hands over her breasts, pinching and pulling, grabbing and slapping, working them over, watching them roll under his fingers, watching her nipples grow hard, and crinkle, turning dark pink. He looked into her eyes, when she could will them to stay open, reading her every response.

"Spread your legs open, slut..." She spread, one leg siding off his lap, bracing herself on the floor. He pressed a finger into her body, above her pubic bone, rolling it around until she jumped.

Smiling at the surprised look in her eyes, he said "Yes, that is your clitoris I just touched. It's big, and it can be reached from inside." Wonder filled her. Here was this man, teaching her something about her own body she didn't even know.

"Since you took your punishment like such a good girl, I think you deserve a reward. But remember, you have to ask, don't cum without permission."

Yeah, sure. She'd see if he could even get her there.

Most men would just rub her clit directly, which would make her want to punch them in the face. It didn't feel good, it was torture. Kudos to them for knowing most women needed their clit played with to cum, she guessed, but that wasn't her. Only she could get herself off clitorally. But she'd mentioned something like that to him, and he seemed like the kind of man who was always taking little mental notes. She didn't think much got past him.

His fingers went back inside her pussy. One, then two, then three... and he found her g-spot, and then... other places, too. But back again to the g-spot and to everything that made her jump and wiggle and moan, until she was tilting her pelvis at him, trying to pump back against his fingers, bucking, riding him. And she felt the pressure build and build and build. She felt the rush inside of her.

Shocked, breathless, she cried out "Please? Please? Pleasepleasepleaseplease?"

"Please what, cockslut?"

"Pleaaaseee may I cum sirrrr?"

"Cum for me," and his fingers pulsed against her g-spot, driving her over the edge. Her body tensed and thrashed as light exploded behind her eyes, and she cried out, a high-pitched wail of release, followed by shuddering aftershocks.

"Thank you... thank you sir," she said.

"I think you have another in you. Don't you, slut?" again he finger fucked her, torturing her breast with his other hand. Her pleasure mounted in crashing waves, rising until she had no choice but to beg again.

"Cum!" he ordered, pulling her nipple hard. He leaned in and took her throat between his teeth, holding her in place, sending her over the edge. Helpless, she felt. Overwhelmed. In ecstasy.

"Well done," he told her, and she felt suffused with warmth. She imagined she was smiling like an idiot. "Good girl," he told her, and bit her ear.

"You still haven't taken care of what you did, though, fuckhole. You made me hard. You will take care of that."

He spun with her still in his arms, tipping her off his lap and onto the raised concrete.

Taking her by the ankles, he stepped off the wooden platform he'd braced his legs on, and dragged her down along the concrete, then walked back to her head.

"What do you want, suckslut?" he asked, unbuckling his belt and opening his pants.

His cock sprang free, and it was lovely, big and thick and throbbing with a distinct head that just screamed to have a tongue swirl around it. The thickness was intimidating and she hated to gag, but she'd trained herself hard to resist that. She'd had no choice. But she loved to please, and she was proud of her progress.

"Please sir, please, may I suck your cock?"

"Good girl," he said, and took her head in his hands, removing all questions, all choice.

She parted her lips, expecting him to just drive himself in, but no. He teased her, her lips, her face. He ran his cock over her like he was marking his territory, his precum smearing across her cheek. The head of his cock swirled over her lips, velvet over pulsing iron. She moaned and flicked her tongue out, tasting him, licking him.

"Yes, that's right cockhole, lick. Lick all the way down," and he slid the shaft of his cock up so that she would lick down him. "Now, lick my balls like a good bitch. That's right. Now suck them."

She felt dirty and nasty and it made her pussy clench. It felt good to be bad.

He pulled his balls out of her mouth and replaced them with his cock, which he slid in, inch by inch, filing her, not stopping until he bottomed out. He paused for a moment and she flailed. He immediately pulled back, gentle, enough that she was breathing again, enough that she didn't gag. He wasn't stopping, though, not at all. He moved her head, up and down his shaft, clearly enjoying the way her tongue ran over him while her lips pressed down. She had been trained to please well, and he was more than willing to teach her what he liked.

Slowly he increased his speed, and after a while he held her head still, and began to fuck her face. In and out, in and out, she felt as though she were a helpless vessel. A face to be fucked. A hole to be used. And now he would cum in her mouth and she would swallow and he would be done with it... but he had made her cum first instead of just fucking her face, and what a wonder that was!

His cock flared and his muscles tightened, she could see his balls were high and tight and prepared herself to swallow as fast as she could, and try to breathe in there somehow...

He froze. Let out a deep breath. Pulled out. What?

"I'm not done with you yet, whore."

She blinked up at him, slowly closing her mouth. Oh god, was he really going to?

"Lie on your side. Back that sweet ass up to the edge here."

He was. He really was. She could hardly breathe, hardly move. She couldn't even think. But then she was rolling, she was moving, her pulse thundered in her ears. He was going to and she wasn't going to stop him, no, she wanted it, wanted him to take her, wanted him to penetrate her, possess her, use her, and fuck her.

He pulled the leg that was on the bottom out, and straddled it, then lifted up her other leg. He was going to take her like that? She felt so exposed. So used. vulnerable, helpless, an object, a toy to callously fuck.

"That's right," he said, reading her thoughts in her eyes, "You're just a piece of fuckmeat for me to get off in, you're a hole for me to use, and I'm going to enjoy you."

His cock was still wet with her spit as he took it in his hand and guided the head into her glistening opening, and then he took her throat in his hands, turning her head so that he could stare into her eyes. His were dark, burning with lust, filled with something bestial, something that would not be denied. He looked like he would devour her.

"I'm going to fuck you however I want, and I'm going to take you hard, like you deserve to be fucked, little slut. And you're going to take it like a good girl. You don't have a choice. You knew this would happen. It was always going to happen." His head popped in, the ridges forcing their way past her ring of muscle, into her soft, warm pussy. She whimpered.

He growled.

He released her throat and slapped her tits, his cock still in her opening. Waiting. So much control. He pulled a nipple. Spanked her ass. And then... then he wrapped his arm around her thigh to brace himself, and he slammed his cock into her, deep and hard, and then pounded her, over, and over, and over again. Ramming into her, bottoming out, each impact shuddering through her body, making her ass shake and her breasts jump. Fast and hard and faster and harder.

She heard something shrieking and howling. She realized it was her. He leaned over her, forcing her legs open wider, and clapped a hand over her mouth.

"Ssssh now, shhhhh, nobody's going to come for you. You're my cockwhore to take, here. My fuckhole. Don't you dare fucking make a sound, little slut." She breathed rapidly through her nose, nostrils flaring. He let go of her mouth and ran his hand down to her chest, now slowly fucking her, but deep. He squeezed a breast, and slapped it, then pulled one nipple after the other, watching her struggle with it, sucking air between her teeth.

"Mmmm," he said, and slapped her breasts again and again, then rose up and grabbed a sore ass cheek, plunging into her hard again. She felt another orgasm rising up inside of her, and started to buck against him again, fucking him back as best she could sideways.

"Don't you dare cum without asking" he growled, and she begged, she pleaded, as he drove her higher and higher and higher.

"Please please please let me cum pleaaaaase sir pleeease!"

He reached down and grabbed the top of her pussy with his hand, squeezing hard, and said "Cum *now*, slut, cum!"

The pain, the violation, drove her over the edge again and she came, trying so hard to not scream, but still, "ah, aah aaaah" it was a strangled cry and her whole body spasmed with the orgasm.

He pulled out suddenly, and she ached with emptiness, wanting him inside her again.

"Please more sir, please?"

"I plan to, slut. Because I want to. On your stomach. Now."

She rolled so she was face down.

"Now put your arms out in front of you, straight out, one hand on top of the other. And don't you dare move. Hold still, like a good fuckhole. You're here to be used. Learn your place, slut."

She shivered and did as he said, her legs dangling, arms stretched before her. His hands gripped her hips and pulled her back a little bit. And held her that way. A breath. Two. Three. Her heart in her throat. Not knowing when it was coming. Not knowing how hard. Helpless, an object to be used.

"Good girl."

Used and savored.

His thumbs spread open her lips, the head of his cock pressed against her pussy, and then he was ramming into her, his hips slapping her ass, his balls bouncing off of her, burying himself to the hilt, slamfucking her over and over and over again. Every thrust of his cock beat her on the inside, and little cries escaped her throat as she felt herself, impossibly, getting closer and closer to cumming again.

Her cunt spasmed and clenched down on his turgid member and he whined out a high pitched "pleeeeeeeease," barely able to form a single word, so lost in her lust and submission.

"Cum!" he growled, and pumped her hard and fast, his cock beginning to twitch, the thrusts becoming erratic. She came, bearing down on him, and she could hear a groan escape him. Suddenly he ripped his cock out of her, dug his fingers into her ass cheek with a trembling hand, and she felt the hot slap of thick liquid splattering over her ass.

Panting, both of them dripping sweat, she felt him lean over her. He ran his hand up and down her back, petting her.

"Good girl, very, very good. That's how you take care of a top you've cock teased, little slut," he whispered in her ear. "Now, back down off that ledge.

Can you stand up?"

She tried, but was a little shaky, so he held on to her and told her to breathe. Wrapping his arms around her, he pulled her close, and she could feel his heart beating in his chest. They breathed together for a while, and then he ruffled her hair. "Well done," he said again.

"Thank you, sir."

He bent down and handed her the shorts and panties he'd pulled off earlier. "You can wear my cum on your ass to remind you of what happens to sluts who tease their boss," he said, smirking.

She shivered and blushed, but smiled up at him. "That's nasty, sir. I... I like it."

"Good girl. Now dress, put yourself together."

She arranged her messy painting clothes as best she could, and looked up into his eyes. "So um. What now?"

"You know," he mused, "I think I'd prefer that window frame in matte. Back to work."

EGO: FREE ME

By Sara the Black

1 Pondering

I've heard people call, label or otherwise justify kink and general forms of BDSM as an escape from normal social constraints as an unconventional form of therapy. My beer habit is arguably way cheaper but there an unattainable height of inner Zen I've never been able to reach otherwise. In Subspace or in Suspension- I'm truly free and unbreakable.

I know it's a bit trendy to have a gender, orientation, and biological preference right now but honestly, my status is just straight up confused.

Being born an intersex individual did not help things one bit. I was thankfully not butchered by the ob/gyn attending staff as much as others like me in the past, I think a lot has to do with awareness of our generation.

"Kit! We're going to be late Bro!" my roommate yelling from downstairs broke me out of my head space. I was standing in front of the full-length mirror in the room usually kept hidden away behind a sheet. I'd been working lately on upper body and chest definition and I think all those late nights of lost sleep gym ratting were finally starting to pay off. I was reluctant to look at the finished tattoo back piece I'd recently had finished up. It was my little secret not yet ready to share.

"On my way, gimme a sec!"

I took one last assessment of myself before yanking on a somewhat clean oversized Hello Kitty tee and grabbing my ratty canvas messenger bag.

Life, to be honest, had become rat race rut. School, work, gym, eat and when possible-sleep. My only escape from it all was Saturday with the Crew. My kinky as hell roommate thinks I'm crazy doing what I do.

2 Where Am I?

It's 6 pm. I'm tuned out hard grooving on some sick base mix as the string of code whizzed by me on the screen. I kept searching for that one string of negative integers that was canceling out the entire line of entry, causing my app update to crash like a methed out Kool-Aid Man in the server sandbox.

Aha!

A light tap on my shoulder popped me out of my groove and I involuntarily shuddered.

"Uh, yeah?" I croaked out, taking off my cushy headphones and looked up trying not to frown.

The Boss-Hole.

"Kit, I need you to finish this up and get the other deliverable done. I want to launch the update and expansion on Monday buddy." Declan did a great Office Space impression, down to the smug lean against my cube divider.

"Uh, no can do Deek. I'm at 40 hours, time now. I can finish up this patch within the time frame but I don't work for free."

"Kit...you are a great asset to this company but there's always someone vying for a cushy position in a..." Declan had the nerve to make air quotes "all-inclusive company. I really need you to show more initiative for the projects you're currently signed up with Buddy!"

"Deek, I don't know what you're getting at but this sounds like I may need to talk to your WIFE in HR." I replied trying very hard not to lose my shit completely.

Declan stepped back, held up his hands in a gesture of truce and cleared his throat.

"Um yeah uh...let's forget we had this talk. Have a good weekend!" That greasy bastard took off like his ass was on fire but it was too late for a sigh of relief.

I clocked out utterly disgusted, having lost my mojo for the day.

I needed an escape from this bullshit, tonight.

3 Who Am I?

I burrowed deeper into my thick hoodie as I stormed out into the cold night. Dolly's version of 'Jolene' queued up on my playlist. I cranked up the volume on my player app and filtered out the passing chaos of the city on a fast walk of a few blocks to my refuge.

It was one of those quirky secrets a city like San Francisco could swallow up and only be a hidden gem to true devotees of the darker side of consensual interludes. Yeah we had our share of sex club, bath houses, fetish bars and porn studios but EGO was a deliciously filthy mix of the best parts of the above with a dedicated cast of burlesque and cirque du freak acts. I reached the quiet unmarked door manned by Tiny, a huge Samoan dude in full Class A's and a Jack Skellington beanie set at an absurd angle on his enormous bald head. He stepped in front of me with a dramatic scowl but those bright green eyes sparkled at some inside joke we've never uttered out loud. I pulled the hoodie back enough to show my face.

"Kit...it's been a while."

"Yeah um...I've been busy with stuff." I glanced up briefly before looking back down at my threadbare Chucks.

"Stuff...yeah. They've been asking about you."

"I owe them an explanation, especially Daddy Mao."

"Yup. Go on in." He grunted, giving me a slap on the back.

I swiped my membership card on the reader. **beep** Finally.

I stashed my gear at coat check and headed straight to the bar. Behind me the house DJ was playing a dub step/witch house mix with seriously cranked up bass. The bartender Katia made eye contact with me and looked momentarily stunned before assuming the usual mask of pleasantry.

"Kit! OMG Babe!!" she had a Jack and Diet Coke (light on ice!) mixed up and slung my way before I had a chance to respond. I smiled and shook my head before chugging round one of liquid courage. She refilled it as soon as the glass hit the highly polished black lacquered counter.

"Thanks." I was relaxing into the next round when Katia looked up and her face immediately went pale. I glanced at the antique mirror behind the bar and studied the crowd behind me.

There in all His splendor, stood Daddy Mao.

Our eyes met via the warped reflection. A finely drawn eyebrow arched briefly before Daddy spun on 5" platform heels and sauntered in an effortless stride into the back hallway.

I slowly finished my drink then slapped down a crisp new c-note on the bar with my glass securing it.

Rolling my shoulders and giving my neck a satisfying crack, I followed Daddy Mao into utter bliss.

---

4 Enlightened

I had some fucking nerves even entering this inner sanctum after violating one of Daddy Mao's most important rules- No play under the influence. I was ready to accept whatever judgment He deemed to bestow on me.

I walked past deep red satin curtains heavily embroidered with an artistic combination of Middle Eastern and Asian motifs. Someone had done some serious redecorating here since the last time I was here months ago. It was sexy, wickedly inviting environment that dared my senses to come to the surface. Tasteful minimalist artwork decorated the walls lit by subtle sconces.

He sat on a lush black leather recliner, long legs crossed. A pair of blue panties briefly teased and delighted my eyes before I caught myself and looked down at the floor.

"Kit, undress and fold your clothes neatly on the shelf to your left. Leave your briefs on until we discuss and revisit our...arrangement." The slightly foreign twang to his deep throaty voice sent an unexpected chill down my back.

"Yes Daddy."

With shaky hands I removed all the layers I hid myself away from with world with, laying myself bare on more levels than I'd be comfortable with in any other situation.

"Come...kneel on the cushion in front of me and let's...catch up and reconnect." Daddy Mao beckoned briefly with a graceful, manicured hand before crossing His legs the other way. I caught myself desperately wanting to kiss those impossible heels. Louboutin, I figured looking at the bright red bottoms. Daddy didn't do counterfeit *or* cheap.

I knelt on the soft bright red pillow in front of him. He lovingly stroked my short unruly of hair, I fought the urge to purr and lean into his touch.

"So, I hope you've grown in your time away from Us. Any new things to disclose, new limits, health concerns?"

"Um...uh..." I stuttered. "No. There's been nothing...n...no one since the l...last time Daddy."

Daddy chuckled quietly to Himself.

"Good Boi." His caress suddenly turned rough as he grabbed my hair and pulled my head back, finally looking me directly in the face. "Good Boi."

"Safeword?"

"Um...Free Me. Safe word is Free Me, Sir."

"Free Me, huh? Someone has had a time of introspection. Good!" He released my head and stood in one fluid motion.

"Alright Boi, get to business." Daddy pulled up His robes and teased my lips with His massive hard on. "Open up; slap my calf if we push your limits."

"Yes, Sir."

I opened up and without preamble he shoved in deep, holding the back of my head in place.

"Such....a....good...Boi!"

I slobbered and gagged trying desperately to please Him. He rode my face without restraint, grabbing a handful of my hair as He came close to climax.

"Look at me!" He ordered in a strained raw voice. "I'm going to cum down that pretty throat of yours Boi."

I gagged hard, drool running down my throat but I doubled my efforts to please Him.

"Aaaaaagh! Good Boi!" He shouted as he came hard, collapsing back into the leather chaise.

There was a moment of silence while we both caught our breath.

Daddy was right there almost immediately after, checking in on me and offering water. I took a small sip, my body still shuddering from the experience.

"Kit, I missed you my dear Boi. Are you ready for the next part?" He looked me in the face, stroking my hair back and giving me a butterfly kiss on my forehead.

"Yes, please Sir."

Nodding, Daddy Mao got up and adjusted his clothes.

"Follow."

I trailed behind the sultry Amazon on shaky legs. In the other room was Mr Singh. He looked me up and down with a condescending snort before motioning me to turn around so he could inspect and sanitize my back.

"Mao, kid got himself some serious back work done. It's healed- I can rig no problem."

"Yes, it's quite an impressive surprise."

"D...done by Cliffton Sir. Only the best for your Boi." I said more excitedly than I meant to.

Mao and Singh both laughed.

"Cute. Stand straight and let me mark off around this little decoration of yours Kid."

I stood slightly chilled as I felt the cold wipes go over my shoulders and back.

"Alright, ready Kit?"

I took a deep breath.

"Ready."

The first hook went in deep, followed by the other. I gasped at the sudden rush of adrenalin.

"Kid has really good skin for this shit Mao. We should add him to the stage show sometime...consent and all this shit aside."

"....we'll see. For now, the Boi has earned his chance to fly. Let's do this."

One final check of the rigging and hooks was done by Singh before he gave a satisfied grunt and stepped back from me.

"Here we go Kit, deep breath."

The lines were slowly cranked up and the slack against the two point hooks tightened up until I was on my toes.

"Go?"

I nodded in a haze. "Go!"

Singh cranked it the rest of the way and I took up to the air.

For that moment frozen in time- Ultimate bliss was mine.

5 Aftercare and Introspection

Daddy and Singh let me hang for about 10 minutes before a check in with me determined it was time to bring me down and let me ride out the high.

Singh let me down gently, removed the rigging and hooks. Daddy Mao brought me warm tea while Singh cleaned and bandaged my wounds. I sat cuddled in a warm blanket at Mao's feet on the pillow while Mr Singh did final cleanup and disposal of all medical waste, removing the black nitrile gloves at the end. He poured himself some tea giving Daddy Mao a thankful nod before seating himself in another chaise.

"Kit?" Came Mao's voice after a long quiet pause. "Are you ok?"

"Y...yes. Thank you Sir."

Daddy Mao smiled warmly and leaned down to give me a peck on my lips. "Good Boi."

I know where I'm loved for who I am. No one has the right to judge me in the end.

ABOUT THE AUTHORS

~ Sumiko Saulson ~

Sumiko Saulson (Mauskaveli on FetLife) is a cartoonist, science-fiction, fantasy and horror writer, editor of Black Magic Women and 100 Black Women in Horror Fiction, author of Solitude, Warmth, The Moon Cried Blood, Happiness and Other Diseases, Somnalia, Insatiable, Ashes and Coffee, and Things That Go Bump In My Head. She wrote and illustrated comics Mauskaveli, Dooky and graphic novels Dreamworlds and Agrippa. She writes for the SEARCH Magazine. The child of African American and Russian-Jewish parents, a native Californian and an Oakland resident who's spent most of her adult life in the San Francisco Bay Area. She is pansexual, polyamorous and genderqueer.

~ Lydia LaRue ~

Lydia is well known for her intricate erotic stories filled with crime, blood, humiliation and a bit of cat play. She can be found drinking coffee with gluten-free banana nut bread at Wicked Grounds where she's a proud Patreon supporter. She currently co-hosts the Kinky Writers Group with Sumiko/Mauskaveli.

~ Mimi Heft (Ouroboros Sings) ~

Mimi Heft (Ouroboros Sings) isn't a writer: she's a musician, graphic designer, businessperson, community organizer, event producer, and foodie; and a romantically monogamous, sexually poly, sapio-semidemisexual hedonist. But not a writer. Nonetheless, she writes deliciously naughty stories featuring her lovers, offered as gifts of affection. Occasionally, she even writes poetry—some of it not so bad. Mimi is not a writer, but words delight her, as does sex, and she shares both with a certain, awkward ebullience.

~ Charlee Verrette ~

Charlee Verrette is a 59-yr old Burlesque Performance artist, Writer. Musician, Actor, Cat Slave who performs as Charlee Debris. They have been performing and creating since 1979 and knew some of the Beats.

~ Serena Toxicat ~

San Francisco-born and bred Serena Toxicat scratches out dark fiction, lyrics, plays and poetry in English and in French. She sings in a Black Catwave band called Protea, and her parallel recording projects include Starchasm. An actor, model-turned-designer, former-pro Domme, NLP life coach, and literary translator, Toxicat leads a scattered, sketchy life and delights in showing her paintings, taking part in LGBTQ+ and kink-focused activities, traveling and collecting tattoos. Serena is a psychic reader, healer, priestess and feline Tarot deck creator. She lived almost 8 years in Paris and traveled to Egypt, where she recorded vocals in the King's Chamber.

~ Francesca Gentille ~

Francesca Gentille (Priestess on Fetlife) is relationship counselor, clinical sexologist, Therapeutic Domme and sacred BDSM educator who is both a Priestess Domme & Tantric Slave. She is the radio host of Sex: Tantra & Kama Sutra, the award winning co-author of *The Marriage of Sex & Spirit*, and the co-director of "The Somatic Sensual Healing Institute." She teaches a Kink Conscious Therapy Certification for Clinicians as well as on Sacred Kink, Ritual BDSM, Therapeutic Kink and Tantric Kink around the world.

~ Lif ~

Lif, born a hyperbolic, living bundle of literary tropes, was meant to be a storyteller since day one. His erotica ranges from taboo fantasies meant to thrill, to more serious pieces meant to raise awareness for emotional and mental health. Outside of erotica, he writes horror-fantasy and science fiction, sings, and produces audio dramas. He is a lifestyle dominant and erotic hypnotist who happily lives as a partial recluse with his cat, experimenting with new mediums of artistic expression.

~ Ev Joy Lokadottr ~

Ev Joy Lokadottr has been a part of the BDSM community for 22 years, and has enjoyed writing for even longer. She is best known for her "how-to" kink lifestyle guides, but has also been known to write an erotic story or three.

~ Merlin Monroe ~

Merlin Monroe, Kaleidoscope Eyes, Seruus Ualerium Tristissima Liber, Pope Uncommon the Dainty, Skunkheart, etc., has 15 names. Fey's a muppet wannabe nun and aspiring trophy wife, longing for both a family and a temple to tend. Identifying as a toy, fear primary sexual identity isn't gay, straight, bi, or pan, but submissive. Fey mostly writes RPG material, poetry, and graphic fiction, and is currently writing a book about DD/ss (Divine Dominance/sacred submission) with Priestess.

~ Kathleen Mahnke ~

Kathleen Mahnke is a kinkstress and writer of stories, author of the Planar Helix series. Maria's proclivities are often derived from Kathleen's kinky escapades. She was a regular part of the Bay Area/San Francisco kink scene before she moved up into the mountains to escape Bay Area rent, only to be caught in the Paradise Camp Fire. She survived the fire but it's been a challenge keeping the creative part of her alive.

~ Sara the Black ~

Sara the Black is an introverted California native hermiting deep in the Santa Cruz Mountains. Proudly multicultural, this primarily Sephardic Jew/Kaldresh Romani was raised in Southern California. A Gender Queer, Asexual, Intersex disabled adult living with multiple chronic illnesses, Sara opted for retirement off-grid with a fiercely independent private contractor/writer companion and neurotic female feline minions. -She- is an unapologetically voracious reader with a healthy appetite for street tacos, good beer, and Hello Kitty

~ Akasha Vampryssa ~

Akasha Vampyrssa is a mysterious bloodsucker who enjoys off-roading, spending time with her sons, grand babies, and her husband. She is from Nevada and when she's not writing, she is out driving across the desert.

~ Max Silver ~

Max Silver (aka Montease Python in Burlesque) is a raunchy rascal rakehell and a ludicrous shaper of words. He hails from San Francisco, and now lives in Oakland. He is part of a Burlesque troupe known as Organized Chaos Oakland, hosting such events as the Lingerie Lounge Open Mic and Organized Chaos Burlesque.

BOOK DESCRIPTION

Dark and seductive, alluring and imaginative, perverse, shocking, and at times hilarious—*Scry of Lust* is an arousing collection of erotica, paranormal romance, sexy poetry, and kinky tales that will spark your desire and quicken your breath. Indulge in the lustful imaginings of this diverse group of writers, all by your naughty self, or share it out loud to entice your lovers. *Scry of Lust* will charm the pants off of you—literally!

Profits from this collection are being donated to the San Francisco AIDSWalk, through SFGoth Team #5015, in memory of Gregory Hug.

The Kinky Writers Group meets weekly at Wicked Grounds Cafe, home of the San Francisco Bay Area's kink and BSDM scene, at the center of the City's Leather & LGBTQ Cultural District. We welcome writers of all experience levels, races, genders, orientations, and sensual proclivities.

Group: fetlife.com/groups/183690

SFGoth AIDSWalk Team: 5105 SFGOTH

This anthology was published by Iconoclast Productions, a San Francisco Bay Area media arts nonprofit organization that works with artists with disabilities, in African American community, produces multicultural programs honoring the African Diaspora, in the homeless community, and in the LGBTQIA+ and Kinky communities.

Contact information:
www.IconoclastProductions.com
sumikoska@yahoo.com

www.ingramcontent.com/pod-product-compliance
Lightning Source LLC
LaVergne TN
LVHW010937100826
845153LV00001B/74
* 9 7 8 0 3 5 9 6 0 5 6 5 1 *